The DAUGHTER *of the* MOON

Also by Gregory Maguire

THE LIGHTNING TIME

The
DAUGHTER
of the
MOON

★

Gregory Maguire

★

Farrar Straus Giroux
New York

Copyright © 1980 by Gregory Maguire
All rights reserved
Printed in the United States of America
Published simultaneously in Canada by McGraw-Hill
Ryerson Ltd., Toronto
First printing, 1980
Designed by Constance Fogler

Library of Congress Cataloging in Publication Data
Maguire, Gregory. The daughter of the moon.
Summary: Twelve-year-old Erikka's opportunities
to step into a picture and experience a
friendship on the other side help her to
solve some pressing problems of an elderly
Russian book dealer.
[1. Space and time—Fiction]   I. Title.
PZ7.M2762Dau   [Fic]   79-25683
ISBN 0-374-31705-4

WITH SPECIAL THANKS TO FRANK PABALAN
FOR HIS HELP, MUSIC, AND FRIENDSHIP

For Anna McAuliff, always

CONTENTS

The DAUGHTER *of the* MOON

Chapter One

THE BOOKSTORE DISASTER

A rain storm had moved in from Lake Michigan and was misting the Chicago streets with spatter and drizzle. The old man at the bookstore window gazed out, and sighed, and picked up his black cat and stroked her.

"I would like to be in a boat, Countess," said the old man, "I could sail right down the middle of Ingoldsby Street, taking riders from corner to corner. You could catch fish—you like the idea?" The black cat purred, oblivious to the old man's words but grateful for his attention. A couple of people were browsing and comparing finds, moving slowly from section to section, drops of rainwater making a trail on the floor as they walked. They didn't seem to be bothered by the old man's talking, so he continued.

"It's like a bad cold, this storm. A virus. Miserable. Be grateful for your warm home, Countess Olga Molokiev; you'd be just wretched as an alley cat." The Countess moved her head under the scratching fingers; then she straightened up and stared out of amber eyes. Down the street two children ran, splashing.

"No regard for puddles or pedestrians," said the old man when the door burst open and the children came crashing in.

"And here we are, I'm absolutely *soaked,*" said the girl, and the boy grinned and squished water out of his shoes.

"Take your wet things off if you've time to stay. Hang up your coats on the hooks by the radiator. Go on, or you'll come down with terrible colds."

"Wait. First, this is my friend Simon Cameron," said the girl to the old man.

"*You* wait—introductions later." The old man pointed meaningfully to the radiator.

They came back then, and the girl made a formal bow and said, "Good afternoon, Mr. Tolyukov."

"Good afternoon, Miss Erikka Knorr." The old man set down the black cat and extended a frail hand.

"Simon Cameron, meet my friend Mr. Tolyukov," said Erikka, mimicking Tolyukov's Russian accent, his slightly chipped syllables and squared sounds. "This is my friend Simon Cameron."

Tolyukov bent low, both to be polite and to see him better.

"Simon. A pleasure indeed," he said, offering his hand. The boy took it, and shook.

"Tol—?" tried Simon.

"Tolyukov. Toll-you-cough. You must pay a Toll if You Cough," explained the bookseller. "Of course, my full name is Modest Mikhailovich Tolyukov—but you don't need all that."

"This is his bookstore," said Erikka.

"May I look around?"

"Of course—go ahead!" said Tolyukov generously. "Are you looking for anything special?"

"I like books about football," said Simon.

"Football, blah," said Erikka.

"To each his own," said Tolyukov mildly. "Over on the far wall, Simon."

Simon turned on a heel and spun off toward that section. He bounded around a corner of shelving and ran right into the woman browser, who dropped the book she'd been inspecting and let out a little yelp.

"Excuse me," said Simon. "I'm so sorry."

"The book," said the woman. "Look at it!" She picked it up and thrust its pages, flapping, at Simon. "You've turned the corners on several pages and ripped the dust jacket. It's no longer in mint condition, and I won't purchase it now. Do watch where you're going. This is a bookstore, not a gymnasium."

"I'm sorry," said Simon again, and disappeared into the stacks.

The offended woman approached the counter. "Really, Mr. Tolyukov. I come here for a little quiet shopping." She put a gloved hand to her brow, indicating a massive headache. "Now you lost a sale just then. This early edition of Frost has been damaged." She ruffled the pages at Tolyukov. "See? A little discipline with your young friends might be in order." She raised her eyebrows and nodded meaningfully toward Erikka. "Now, tell me: any luck in obtaining those essays we've talked about?"

"I'm keeping my eyes open, Mrs. Pruitt," said Mr. Tolyukov. "I've heard a few rumors of one coming on the market soon."

"I rely on you," said Mrs. Pruitt, smiling. "You've been good to us so far. Also: I'm looking for a volume of nursery rhymes to give my niece."

"Just by the window, bottom shelf," said Tolyukov.

"Browler," called Mrs. Pruitt. "Come look at the nursery rhymes with me." Mr. Pruitt disengaged himself from a thick volume of Macaulay and joined his wife by the window. He was large, attired in a monumental tweed coat. The nursery books looked like postage stamps in his thick hands.

"Who are *they?*" whispered Erikka.

"Browler and Regina Hexler Pruitt." Tolyukov leaned close to Erikka. "Their business helps keep this place going. Very wealthy, important people. A bit stuffy, too, if the truth be told." He smiled one of his wrinkled smiles, looking like an old, old frog.

Erikka was one of Tolyukov's favorite persons. She was twelve, and alternately shy and forthright. She'd been coming in the bookstore to talk to Tolyukov for several years now; she was bright, and the seventy-year difference in their ages didn't concern either of them very much.

"I have a reason for coming today," she said seriously, opening her book bag on the counter. "I have a favor to ask."

Tolyukov waited patiently.

The girl drew a paper package out of her satchel and unwrapped it. On the counter she set a simple, clear blue vase. Even with the afternoon light so filtered by rain, even among the somewhat dingy and dusty shelves and stalls of the bookstore, the blue vase glowed, light spinning around its edges and curves, pale blue, cerulean, midnight blue; Tolyukov and Erikka as dwarfed dark figures were reflected in the curving neck.

"It is a beautiful piece of glass," said Tolyukov.

"It belonged to my first mother, and when she died, my father gave it to me," Erikka said. "I love it."

"But why is it here?"

"Well, it's a complicated story," Erikka said. "My Aunt Kristina—my first mother's sister—is coming to stay with us for a couple of weeks, so my second mother has decided that Aunt Kristina will sleep in the little girls' room. That means that Inga and Annie are going to move in with me for two whole weeks! I don't know if I can stand it. They are so sloppy and crazy. I'm afraid that they'll break it, even if I wrap it up and put it in a drawer. So will you keep it for these—"

"We'll make this purchase now," interrupted Mr. Pruitt. He put several books down on the counter, next to the blue vase.

"I'll be right with you," said Tolyukov. "Continue, Erikka."

"I would just like you to keep it, please, until the girls

move back to their own room," Erikka said quickly.

"If you don't mind, Mr. Tolyukov? Thank you," said Mr. Pruitt, a bit louder.

"Yes, of course," said Tolyukov. He picked up the blue vase and handed it back to Erikka. "You can take this to the back room, Erikka, and put it on the table."

"Thank you," she said.

"Cash or charge, now?" asked Tolyukov.

"Umm. Charge it," said Mr. Pruitt. "And can you give us a quick idea of this month's bill?"

Mr. Tolyukov took a notebook from a drawer. "It's quite a bit," he said. "That pair of British Bibles, and the Waverley novels; they're all on this current bill." His finger indicated the amount at the end of a column of figures.

"A sizable bill, this one," said Mr. Pruitt.

"A payment at your earliest convenience would be appreciated," said Mr. Tolyukov. "You know I operate on a shoestring budget, with very little extra capital."

"Regina, write Mr. Tolyukov a check for five thousand," said Mr. Pruitt. Mrs. Pruitt obliged by fumbling in her bag for a minute. Erikka and Simon began playing with the Countess, spinning a ball of aluminum foil along the floorboards between them, the Countess chasing it madly.

"You do baby-sitting as well as book procuring, eh?" laughed Browler Pruitt, nudging Mr. Tolyukov in the ribs.

"These are my friends, Erikka and Simon." Mr. Tolyukov moved out of nudging reach.

"The date, dear," asked Regina, scribbling out a check. Her husband told it to her.

The Countess cavorted after the ball. Erikka scooped it up and tossed it to Simon, but it bounced on a shelf and landed on the counter. The Countess flew up after it, but became confused, and batted at the most obvious toy: Regina Hexler Pruitt's rosewood pen.

"She scratched me!" screamed Mrs. Pruitt, and hit the Countess over the head with the convenient battered volume of Frost.

"Mrs. Pruitt!" said Mr. Tolyukov. The Countess streaked into the back room.

"Really, Mr. Tolyukov, cats and children crawling around here! I'd thought you maintained a more professional business." Mrs. Pruitt had been obviously frightened. She jabbed a finger down on the countertop to make a point and broke off a piece of scarlet fingernail. "I can take my business elsewhere at the drop of a hat."

"Would you like me to drop it for you?" said Simon in a low voice to Erikka. But Mrs. Pruitt heard him. She scooped up her checkbook and purchases and her husband's arm, and churned angrily, wordlessly, out the door. It slammed behind her.

"Oh, no," said Simon.

"The check," said Tolyukov. "She didn't sign the check. It's no good unless she signs it."

"Oh, no," said Simon. "I didn't mean—"

"Oh, no," said Erikka, caught up.

"Well," said Tolyukov. He sighed. His ancient shoulders

sloped like a hill leaning forward. But then he smiled. "Let's have some tea and forget about it."

"Are you going to be able to pay your bills?" said Erikka bluntly.

"Who knows? Of course I am. Don't worry about it," said Tolyukov. "Here, do you want to make us all some tea?"

"It's all our fault!" cried Erikka.

"More mine than yours," Simon said, sniffing mightily. "I was the one who asked if she wanted her hat dropped."

"She's an excitable woman, and everyone's cross because of the weather. Do forget it. Erikka, why don't you make us a nice hot cup of tea?"

"Maybe if we apologize," said Simon.

"On bended knee," said Erikka.

"Roses?" suggested Simon.

"Stop your worrying," said Tolyukov. "A woman so rude isn't worth the time it takes to discuss her. So just forget it. Or out you go, into the rain."

"Just like you," said Erikka, a wave of tears starting. "You'll be evicted, probably, for not paying rent. Out on the curb with all your fine old books in piles around you."

"TEA!"

Erikka leaped up and ran to fill the kettle.

Tolyukov slowly sat down in his rocker. His whole home was this back-room space to his store on Ingoldsby Street—a bathroom and a large room with a bed and a table, a few chairs, and a stove and sink and small refrig-

erator. At the foot of his bed was an old red lacquered
chest, with painted flowers and dragons on it. He had
brought it with him when he had come from Russia. A
long, long time ago.

Tolyukov shook his head and looked at Simon. The
boy was very thin. Thin enough to slip through a crack
in the floorboards.

"Put out a cracker or two and some jam," Tolyukov
said to Erikka.

Tea kettle on, cups out, saucers out, tea bags arranged
in the cups in a similar fashion, their tags all pointing east
—Erikka was of an orderly mind. She swung to the cabinet
for saltines. She knew where everything was in this back
room, from the food in the closet to the Bible at the bedside table to the painted chest Tolyukov sometimes used
as a footstool. In that chest he kept precious letters and
personal treasures, he had told Erikka.

Why can't my house be small and neat, thought Erikka
grumblingly. Just enough room for two chairs by the fireplace, a table for tea, a bed and a sink and a wardrobe. Instead of being crowded and noisy and long, filled with the
debris that follows the trail of the Three Terrors.

I would like to have a parakeet for company, thought
Erikka. Or a toucan, like the one in the Lincoln Park Zoo.
Or perhaps even a cat, or a turtle or two. I would be fine
and happy, all alone, all all alone, she sang to herself. I
could have paintings on the walls.

In a businesslike fashion she poured the boiling water

into the teacups and set the cups on a tray showing the onion domes of St. Basil's in Moscow, and took the tray and tea and crackers and jam over to Tolyukov and Simon, who were sitting, not saying anything. Simon was rubbing his eyes.

"I love your house," said Erikka.

"So did he," said Simon darkly.

"Now you two, please," Tolyukov pleaded. "Give an old man a break."

Erikka realized Tolyukov didn't want to talk about it now. She gave Simon a cup of tea and looked meaningfully into his eyes, as if to say, We'll talk about this later, outside.

"I hate tea," said Simon conversationally.

"Drink it," said Tolyukov. "It's good for you."

The Countess padded softly by, and then leaped up on the windowsill, to look out the back window into the alley. Through the screen of rain little could be seen of the trash cans and old bedsprings and fruit crates from the market next door. But the Countess stared anyway.

"Now, tell me about your aunt," said Tolyukov, sipping tea.

Erikka put her cup down. "Her name is Kristina Angstrand. She's my first mother's younger sister. Her hair is long and golden and fine, not like mine, all brown, the color of dust. She came a couple of years ago, for the funeral, when my first mother died. She came when my father married my second mother, too. She lives in Boston, I think. She's an illustrator."

"A what?" asked Simon.

"An illustrator. She draws pictures for books and magazines. In two years, when I'm fourteen, my second mother said maybe I could take a bus all the way to Boston to visit her! She's not married."

"Why is she coming?" asked Tolyukov. "Friendly visit?"

"Oh, partly. But there's some editor she's meeting here in Chicago, and she'll be working on a book for a couple of weeks. When it's all over, she'll go back to Boston."

"I have an uncle," Simon said brightly. "John. Uncle John. He came once on visiting day and said he'd like to adopt me, but his wife wouldn't let him."

"Are you an orphan, Simon?" Tolyukov asked.

"No," Simon said. "My father is widowed and doesn't think he can raise me all by himself."

"You should see the Dearborn School for Boys. Pure hell," stated Erikka.

"Your language, my friend!" said Tolyukov, alarmed. "It can't be all that bad!"

"It's lousy," agreed Simon, pretending to sip some tea. "But I don't care that much. I just get out as often as I can. The boys there are okay, but it's nicer to know real people who have families."

"You live at the school?" Tolyukov asked.

"Ugh. If you can call it living."

"*I* would call it torture," said Erikka. "They have rules for every minute of the day, every day of the week. It's like being in prison. Seven o'clock, wake up; seven-fifteen, eat breakfast; seven-thirty-five, brush your teeth; seven-forty-five, classes begin—"

"Don't you live like that?" Tolyukov asked Erikka. "On a schedule?"

"Sort of. But it's flexible. And I only have to contend with the Three Terrors. Simon shares a room with nineteen other boys! And they all have to do the same thing at the same time! Three o'clock, homework! Four o'clock, chores! Four-thirty, recreation!"

"Surely you have no objection to recreation?" Tolyukov asked, eyebrows raised.

"When you *have* to do it? Every day except Sunday? Or else you get punished? A place where you have to sign up for either Ping-Pong or billiards or darts, where you have to play whether you want to or not, and where they keep records, permanent score sheets forever, year in year out?" Erikka was talking faster and faster, waving her spoon around, splattering little drops of tea on all three of them. "It's like a war camp!"

"Hush, my excitable friend," said Tolyukov. "Is it so bad, Simon?"

"Every bit," said Simon with relish. "I hate it."

"Well." Tolyukov leaned back in his rocker. Such a lot of things to think about! He rocked back and forth a bit. Then he looked at his watch.

"It's ten minutes of five, Simon," he said. "What do they have programmed for you today?"

"I should be writing a letter to my father now," admitted Simon.

"In fact, you're not supposed to be out today," guessed the old man.

"Oh, I know all the tricks of escaping without detection," Simon assured him. "I've been there for four years."

"But the letter to your father?" asked Tolyukov.

"Why should I write my father? He never has time to write back. But the proctor makes me write him, anyway." Suddenly Simon looked very angry. "What a waste of time! Who wants to write letters that aren't going to be answered."

"Simon," Tolyukov said softly, "are you going to get in trouble when you get back this afternoon?"

"I don't care if I do."

"He might," Erikka said eagerly. "He probably will. Terrible trouble. He won't be able to talk to the other boys until tomorrow morning. He'll have to scrub the hall floor with a brush."

"Hmmm. Perhaps I shall walk you back to the school this evening. After all, I've nothing better to do," said Tolyukov.

"Simon, you haven't drunk your tea," Erikka noticed.

"I don't like tea. I hate it," Simon said, and no one forced it on him.

Tolyukov wiped his mouth on his sleeve and looked at the blue vase. "I think, Erikka, there should be some sort of exchange," he said thoughtfully. "If I take something of yours, you should take something of mine."

"Why?"

"Collateral. It's good business procedure. Then if I

should break your vase, God forbid, you'd have the right to keep what you borrowed from me. It's how things are done."

"But you're not going to break it!"

"Of course not. Nevertheless, I insist on a fair exchange. I will loan you something valuable of mine until your aunt goes back to Boston and you can take the vase home without fear of your sisters smashing it."

"The Three Terrors are trained to destroy. They're qualified wreckers," said Erikka.

Tolyukov laughed, pulling himself to his feet. He shuffled over to his chest and opened it. Erikka had never seen the inside before, although Tolyukov had told her what he kept there. Nobly, she restrained herself from leaping up to investigate—but she did lean and arch to see as well as she could from where she was. It wasn't too exciting. Everything was wrapped in old newspaper. Tolyukov pulled out a package about as long as a loaf of bread, only narrower. He held it out to Erikka.

"Unwrap it now," he said.

The sheets of newspaper fell away under her quick fingers. The thing was heavy, knobby, intricate.

An ancient sword handle? A Baroque door stop?

"A candlestick," Tolyukov said. "From Russia. From a little country church, the Church of St. Nicholas. One day I was walking with the Countess Olga—only, of course, this was after the Revolution, as you know, Erikka, and the title did not hold any more—and it began to rain, and we ran up into the church for cover. Neither of us lived in that town; we did not know the priest. As we sat there, silently, in the golden-gray light, suddenly a door at the back of the choir was flung open and a mad-looking priest came tumbling in. Later we found he truly was mad; he had lost his mind during the Revolution. He ran to us, carrying this candlestick, and begged me to take it, to keep it safe from the armies. 'They will steal, plunder,' he shrieked, 'and the fires of the sanctuary must not be dimmed!' The Countess was quite shaken; she kept pulling on my sleeve and whispering, 'Take it, Modest, and let's go!' So I did. The priest calmed down and began to sing quietly, walking away. I was going to leave the candle-stick by the door—I didn't think I had a right to it—but as we were leaving, the Countess said, 'You promised to take it. So you must.' And so I did. Of course, I didn't know that when I went to America that same year, I would lose touch with the Countess. But I did keep it, all these years."

"How wonderful!" Erikka breathed.

"Your sisters couldn't hurt it unless they pushed it out the window," Tolyukov said. "Now, I think we should be getting along. It's almost time for your dinner, Erikka, and I'm going to close up early since it's been such a slow day. Maybe I'll walk Simon home a bit, since I've some letters to mail and want to get out, even if it means get-ting wet."

"Do you love it here, Simon?" Erikka asked as they

were all struggling into raingear. "Even though it's only your first time?"

"Yes," said Simon.

"You mustn't put him on the spot, Erikka," Tolyukov admonished her. "Give him time to form his own opinions."

"I'd like to hear more about the Countess," Simon suggested.

"So would I," Tolyukov remarked dryly.

"And you didn't even get a chance to meet Francisco," Erikka complained as she put the candlestick in a paper bag. "You can meet him some other time, if you come again, if you want to come again, if you ever *can* come again."

"Maybe," Simon said.

Tolyukov held open the back door for Simon and Erikka. The rain came driving in, splashing on the whiskers of the Countess, who indignantly recoiled, looked about her to see if anyone had seen the outrage, and then leaped to the table to finish the tea Simon had left.

Chapter Two

THE SUDDEN
PAINTING

At a corner, they parted ways, and Erikka stood for a moment to watch Mr. Tolyukov and Simon Cameron go off down the street, the older one skirting puddles carefully, the younger splashing right through. She was glad Tolyukov was walking with Simon; she liked them both and wanted them to like each other.

She turned and ran the other way. This was her street; it was ugly, ugly, godawful ugly. Erikka didn't know what godawful meant, because God couldn't be awful, even if he tried, but the phrase had a nice convincing ring to it, and it sounded as if it described Merriam Street. Ugly shops, ugly trash cans, ugly signs and lights, ugly people. The crabby old lady who ran the laundromat on the corner had once thrown Erikka and the Three Terrors out into the cold of a blizzardy January day. (Erikka had lost her key to the apartment and they couldn't get in.) "We do laundry here, not baby-sitting," the laundromat lady had tartly stated, and Erikka's pleas had been useless. Ever since, Erikka had hated her with a vengeance, the way she hated the butcher for calling her "my little girlfriend," and the vacuum-cleaner repairman for burning her once with a cigarette (it was by accident, but all he had said was, "Watch where you're goin', girlie"). She could imagine them all banding together on windy nights, in the basement of one of their shops, calling themselves the Merriam Street Monsters and deciding on new and insidious ways to antagonize the neighborhood children.

But Erikka would never side with most of the children who lived above the shops, either, even though they were all mutually disliked by the merchants. Most of the kids were jerks and troublemakers, and Erikka avoided the kids and the grownups with the same care. She had perfected an "I'm thinking-of-something-important-so-don't-bother-me" look, which she wore whenever she was on her street.

Aunt Kristina, Aunt Kristina, coming tonight! she trumpeted to herself as she ran past the laundromat, the butcher shop, the vacuum-cleaner place. She reached the Merriam Deli and looked in. Florry, the waitress, was drumming a pencil against her front teeth in a bored fashion; business was slow on rainy evenings. Erikka rapped on the glass and waved. Florry waved back. Then Erikka unlocked the door on the right side of the deli entrance and went upstairs.

The Three Terrors were playing with cars in the front room.

"Erikka?" called her mother. "You're late. It's five-fifteen. You'll have to dry dishes tonight for Inga; she set the table for you."

"That's not fair! Drying is more work than setting a table!" Erikka protested, and then shut her mouth quickly. She was older than Inga, she ought to be doing the more taxing job.

"Brum brum, brum brum," droned Bengt, being a motor.

"Brum brum, brum brum," squealed Inga and Annie, crashing their cars into his.

Erikka was twelve, the oldest. She had lots of chores, but she also was allowed to go out in the afternoons without having to announce where she was going. This was the best thing about being the oldest one.

Inga was nine, and, to Erikka, dismissable.

Annie was four. She sometimes reigned as Queen of the House, and everybody obeyed her until they got sick of it, after which she sulked. She was the one that visitors always said was a looker. Inga and Erikka were insulted by this; they surveyed each other critically in the bathroom mirror. Erikka said Inga's nose wasn't so terribly snub. Inga said Erikka's hair wasn't *really* dull, more the color of dead leaves than mouse color. But they weren't convinced.

Bengt was two and a half. He was too young to remember their first mother, who had died soon after he was born. It was too early to tell about Bengt; his allegiances altered daily. He would be your best friend one day and steal your lunch cookie the next. When he was with Inga and Annie, though, he generally caught some of their mischievousness, and that was why Erikka called them the Three Terrors.

"Brum brum," Bengt crooned, running a plastic car along the floor and up the side of the sofa.

"Brum brum! Crash crash!" shouted Annie, trying to drive her car down the neck of Bengt's shirt.

"Brum brum, errrrrrk!" Inga propelled her car at breakneck speed along the precipice of the coffee-table edge.

"Really, Inga," said Erikka. "I can understand Annie and Bengt playing cars. But you?"

"Oh, Mrs. Grownup, sorry if it bothers you. Here's how you drive a car. Putt putt putt putt—six miles an hour," said Inga.

"Oh, yeah? I can drive faster than you," Erikka challenged. She picked up a discarded toy and whirled it along the coffee table. It passed Inga's car and flew off into space.

"Oh, yeah? That's kid stuff." Inga sniffed. She did the same, but her car flew up in the air and hit the television set.

"Kid stuff!" screamed Annie happily, and she threw her car in the air, too. It hit a white bottle that stood in a place of honor on the mantel of the boarded-up fireplace. Horrified, Erikka leaped across the room. It was their second mother's prize possession. Just as it rolled off the shelf, Erikka caught it.

"Bad girl," said Erikka sternly. "That is Mommy's *favorite thing* in the world. You shouldn't throw things in the house."

"Naughty girl," Inga added. "Naughty." She shook her finger.

Annie began to cry.

"Brum, brum," Bengt murmured, heading on his hands and knees toward the kitchen.

"Supper is ready," said their mother. "Wash up."

When they were seated, and grace had been said, Mrs. Knorr ladled bean soup out into all their bowls and passed around bread. She was a solid woman, with a thick strong back and impressive arms, and a face that was, thought Erikka, somewhat plain. She looked as if she never had time to get fixed up, which was understandable because the new Mrs. Knorr was *always* working. She taught four nights a week, courses in the history of architecture over at the university, and when she wasn't teaching she was marking papers, or making stew and marking papers simultaneously, or doing the laundry for old Mr. Volgarakis next door, who couldn't get out because his legs were as stiff as plaster. Mrs. Knorr was unstoppable.

When she had first moved in, after having married Erikka's father last fall, she had slipped right into the routine of things as if she'd always lived there. Inga and Annie and Bengt almost didn't notice that their new mother was preparing the meals and handing out quarters for church instead of Erikka. But Erikka was prepared to be aloof, faithful forever to the memory of her own mother, Astrid Angstrand Knorr, her real mother, her dead mother; and this took so much energy that it was a relief to be served meals instead of serving them. The new Mrs. Knorr was so busy with chores and her work and the general commotion of a household that she didn't seem to notice Erikka's staunch silences.

Like now. There she was, calmly breaking Bengt's bread into digestible pieces, oblivious to Erikka's private rebellion. Erikka looked at her critically, across the bowls and plastic drinking glasses on the table.

If only she would wear a rose in her hair, or maybe a lace shawl on her shoulders; anything to decorate what was essentially a simple woman. But Mrs. Knorr wore pants most of the time, and her husband's heavy jackets; she didn't even dress up for church on Sunday. Now, expecting company, she wore her normal workday clothes, with a little ceramic rose pin as her only concession to festivity.

"You're dawdling, Erikka," Mrs. Knorr said. "Did you have something to eat this afternoon?"

"No," said Erikka. "Oh, yes, I did. Tea at the bookstore." Erikka didn't want to tell her mother what had happened that afternoon. She had to think about it for a while.

"Mommy, where did you get that white bottle in the living room? And would you be mad if it got broke?" Inga asked.

"Why, you know I would," their mother said. "It belonged to my mother. It's an old-fashioned barber's bottle. In the old days, barbers kept their lotions in handsome bottles like that one. I took it from my mother's home when she died last Thanksgiving. You remember that? The time I left for a week and Florry came upstairs and made supper for you every night?"

"She kept making eggs," said Erikka. "Every night, eggs. Scrambled, fried, poached . . ."

"Eggs on toast, eggs on ham," said Inga.

"Eggs and jam," said Erikka.

"Eggs and Spam," suggested Inga.

"All right!" Mrs. Knorr laughed. "But you remember, I see. I came home that week with that white bottle; it was a favorite of hers and it means a lot to me." She suddenly looked a little wary. "Has anything happened to it, Inga?"

"No, no!" said Inga. "Nearly. But not."

"Woe betide the hapless soul," said Mrs. Knorr, threatening them with the ladle. "You'd be grounded for ten years."

"Your mother's dead and our mother's dead," said Annie suddenly, grinning. "Does that mean we're twins, Mommy?"

"Sort of," said Mrs. Knorr.

"I wonder if they know each other in heaven," Inga pondered.

"There's no doubt!" cried Erikka.

"Eggses," said Bengt, who was too young to keep up with the general conversation.

"Is Aunt Kristina dead?" asked Annie.

"No, dear. More soup, girls? Bengt, stop driving your car in the soup! Annie, take that car from him."

"Bad Bengt! Bad bad boy!" Annie grabbed his car. Bengt bawled.

"Really, there's no need to be so rough," said Inga

coolly. "Mommy, what time is Aunt Kristina getting here?"

"Her plane arrives at seven, and she'll take a taxi into town. So maybe eight o'clock or so."

"Erikka, can Toby come into our room?" Annie asked. Toby was the rocking horse.

"No. And it's *my* room. You're only a guest."

"So will Toby be."

"So will Toby not be."

"Then neither will I."

"Good. You can sleep in the hall."

"Erikka!" said Mrs. Knorr.

"Well, there won't be any room, Mommy! Toby, and two cots, and my bed, and my desk and dresser. It'll be like climbing a range of mountains to get into bed tonight."

"I am no mountain," said Inga, affronted.

"Mountain!" sang Bengt, dropping from his chair to go climb on Mrs. Knorr's lap.

"Inga, Erikka, would you be good girls and clear the table? I've got my bundle weighing me down," said their mother.

"I'll help, too!" shouted Annie, and pushed a soup bowl off the table, smashing it on the floor. Erikka shivered, but it was a shiver of relief, to think that the blue vase that had belonged to her first mother was at Tolyukov's, safe from the destructive powers of the Three Terrors.

Chicago is not a beautiful place, thought Erikka as she dried the dishes alone in the kitchen. Why Aunt Kristina would come, even for a job, is a source of wonder to me. It is a horrid, ugly place, with its squat brick buildings all crowded together like so many kernels on a cob of corn. There is no light, no loveliness; I never see anyone who looks as if they might enjoy beautiful things.

Except Tolyukov, of course. And Francisco de Medina. But that is only two—counting me, three—in a whole city! Countable on one hand, with a thumb and a finger left over!

Erikka tried to be fair as often as possible. Dutifully, as she stacked the bowls in the cabinet, she went through a quick list of people she knew, so as not to think ill of anyone if she could help it. In her own family, the Three Terrors cared only about food and fighting with each other and who was going to get to sit in the good chair for nightly television.

And, Erikka thought, her second mother would as soon see a blank wall as a painting. She would as soon listen to the noise from the traffic on Merriam Street as turn on a radio or listen to a record. A day didn't pass that Erikka didn't stifle a complaint at her mother's dull, functional clothes. Monday through Friday: housekeeping all day, and classes and meetings at night. How tedious. And on the other nights, did she dress up in flaming red gowns and dance the night away, carefree, silly, wild? No. She did laundry and mending, and went to bed early with an orange and a thick book with lots of close print.

In all justice, Erikka thought, starting on the glasses, there was nothing so romantic or passionate in her other mother, either. Before she had died, she had done sewing and dusting and those things, too.

And Daddy—it was so hard to tell. He had a job selling textbooks all over the country and was rarely home. Every other weekend he came home, and he took them all out, to the lake, or to Lincoln Park or the Brookfield Zoo or the Museum of Science and Industry, or, best, the Chicago Art Institute. Sometimes their mother would come and sometimes not. But when she did, she was always too busy with Bengt to notice the paintings. And Daddy was the same.

Erikka's spirits sank as her list went on. Florry, who minded them on the nights their mother worked, didn't care about much but her hairdo and her boyfriends. The teachers at school took a dim view of wonderful things, more fascinated by the rigors of training in grammar and arithmetic. Her best friend in school was Doreen O'Donald. Doreen's wealthy parents sent her to art class, to piano lessons, to dancing school, and Doreen hated it all. She energetically resisted any attempts at cultural improvement. It was a crying shame, Erikka thought. Here was Doreen complaining about scales and keys and bourrées and perspective and light and shadow, and Erikka was stuck in a family whose only interest in anything beautiful was a stroll in the park to see the squirrels.

Once at lunch Doreen had moaned about a poetry reading that her parents had dragged her to the night before. Erikka was entranced. "Oh," she had cried, "what did they look like, the poets? Do you remember anything they said? What were their poems about? Did they look happy or sad?" But Doreen had spent the whole evening on the fire escape, trying to throw twigs into an open garbage can in the alley below. Erikka almost wept at the injustice of it all.

The merchants of Merriam Street were all so engrossed in commerce that they had no time to consider the finer things in life. Or so Erikka assumed.

Thank God for Tolyukov, Erikka stubbornly thought, drying the spoons, and determined to end her ruminations on a positive note. If it weren't for him and Francisco, I would be alone in this dark and fortress-like city, Tolyukov with his love of music and literature, his quoting poetry, his stopping Francisco on his way past and asking him for a melody on his violin. That bookstore is like a church to me, thought Erikka: words to listen to and think about, music sometimes to push the words towards other and grander meanings, friends to smile at and feel comfortable with, and all of that somehow adding together, making a total feeling that was larger than the good feelings of the separate parts . . .

"Come kiss me good night! Tuck me in!" Annie was screaming from the back bedroom, the bedroom that Erikka usually had to herself.

"Why doesn't Erikka have to go to bed now?" asked Inga sullenly, pulling the sheet modestly up to her neck as Erikka and Mrs. Knorr came in the room.

"Because she's twelve, and you're nine, and that's that. Did you say your prayers?"

"No."

Erikka knelt down with her mother, to say prayers with Inga and Annie, but as the words were coming out she furtively glanced around the room. It was a mess. Annie *had* dragged Toby in, as far as he would fit inside the door; Inga had piled up all her clothes and stuffed animals on the dresser. The ornate candlestick Tolyukov had loaned to Erikka was pushed aside. The few books Erikka owned were sprawled on the floor . . . those precious books Tolyukov had given her, books about magic and poetry and hard-to-believe adventures, shoved to the floor . . .

"Amen," they said, except Erikka, who sprang to her feet and said, "Inga, you little brat," and hit her on the knee.

"Stop that," said Mrs. Knorr.

Inga said, "Goodnight, dear Mother and darling little Annie. Oh, and I almost forgot. Good night, Toby."

"Good night, Erikka," said heart-of-gold Annie.

"Sleep tight, girls, and don't let the bugs bite," said Mrs. Knorr, which set them off in a chorus of squealing in mock pain. Erikka picked up her books and looked through them. A few pages were bent. Inga would pay with her life if *she* had anything to say about it.

"When's Daddy coming home again?" asked Erikka, when she and her mother were sitting together in the living room, waiting for the cab that would bring Aunt Kristina from the airport.

"Now, Erikka, you know he was just home this past weekend. It'll be about two weeks from now."

Erikka looked around the living room. The precious barber's bottle gleamed, reflected the lamplight by which Mrs. Knorr was sewing. It is the only nice thing in this room, thought Erikka, and it almost got smashed to smithereens.

She was restless. She knew if she just sat there her mother might suggest that she go to bed and greet Aunt Kristina in the morning. But Erikka wanted to stay up. So she went and found a pencil by the phone and a piece of paper, and started to draw.

"What're you drawing?" asked Mrs. Knorr.

Erikka didn't answer. The barber's bottle on the page didn't look anything like the actual bottle, and she was embarrassed by it.

"Or *are* you drawing?" said Mrs. Knorr, her eyes on her sewing.

"It's hard to tell, I know," said Erikka fiercely, "whether I'm drawing or scribbling a pen around to make sure what color the ink is."

"Let me see," said Mrs. Knorr.

Erikka held up the paper. "It's your famous bottle. Looks as if Annie did it."

"I heard that!" screamed Annie from the bedroom. "I can draw gooder than you, anyway!"

"It's *better,* not gooder, and go to sleep," called Mrs. Knorr.

"It's not better, *I'm* better," yelled Annie.

"And I'm absolutely rotten," said Erikka, crumpling the page in one hand and throwing it on the floor.

"Pick that up. It looked very nice, Erikka."

Erikka retrieved the paper and threw it in the trash. Then she flopped down on the sofa and covered her eyes with her hands.

After a while, she said, "Did you ever hear anyone play the violin?"

"Yes," said her mother.

"What did you think?"

"What did I think?" Mrs. Knorr put down her sewing for a minute and then picked it up again. "I thought it sounded like an ambulance siren."

"Oh, Mommy," said Erikka, despite herself.

"What?" Mrs. Knorr seemed genuinely surprised.

"That's so *terrible.* An ambulance siren! Why didn't you think it was *beautiful?*"

"Because it wasn't. It was my brother Bruce, when he was thirteen. He hated to play. Eventually he threw his violin in the lake and told my mother it had been stolen. She didn't believe him for a minute."

"Oh." Erikka was silenced for a minute.

"Did you ever hear a good violinist?" she asked.

"Erikka, what's this sudden interest in violin music? I don't understand."

"Well, I know a guy who plays, that's all. And it sounds like real music, all flowing and sad and romantic, or else wild, like a dance or a war or something. I just wondered if you ever felt that."

"Not often. I don't particularly enjoy violin music. No one who had to live with Bruce's aggrieved practicing could. Where did you hear a violinist?"

"One lives next door to Mr. Tolyukov's store, and he plays for Mr. Tolyukov and me sometimes." Erikka was sorry she had brought the subject up. But just then the doorbell rang.

Erikka was up, out into the hall, where the boots were heaped in a cardboard box, down the red-brown stairs (the brown part was where the paint had worn off and the wood showed through), and then she was tugging at the heavy door and throwing herself at her aunt.

When they climbed the stairs to the Knorrs' apartment, both of them lugging suitcases, Mrs. Knorr met them at the top of the stairs and gave Aunt Kristina a hug and a kiss. That's funny, because they're not real sisters, thought Erikka suddenly, they're not related at all. She is the sister of my first mother. But her thoughts were interrupted. Annie and Inga were standing coyly in the doorway to the bedroom hall. They knew they shouldn't be up, but their impish smiles were too much for Mrs. Knorr.

"All right, you little tricksters, come in and give your Aunt Kristina a kiss, but then it's right back to bed, do you hear me?"

They hurried in, kissed and beamed, and left giggling.

"You're looking fine," said Erikka's mother as Aunt Kristina took off her coat. And for once, Erikka approved of her mother's judgment. Aunt Kristina was not old; she was probably not yet thirty. She had a wondrous rich sweep of golden hair looped on her head in a sort of rope, and she held her head as if she were proud of the thoughts it contained. Like statuary, thought Erikka of her limbs; not like mine, short and fat and oddly-shaped, but like the statuary they have in the courtyards of museums. And her clothes! Great sweeping reaches of wool, great draping folds of some material Kristina had woven herself, with threads of blue and green and silver and white. Clothes fit for a queen, really, and that enviable golden hair made an entirely suitable crown, a natural one. Erikka was enthralled, just standing there looking at her. I sure wish I could bring her to school to show Doreen what a real LADY looks like. But then Doreen wouldn't care.

Aunt Kristina and Mrs. Knorr started talking and talking and talking. Erikka expected this and didn't mind. She just sat, grateful to be allowed to hear her aunt's nice rippling voice, with all the interesting words she used, and all the fascinating places she had been to. Every so often she would turn and smile at Erikka.

"Goodness! Tea or coffee—I completely forgot. What would you like?" Mrs. Knorr bounded up. "Or we have some beer in the fridge, I think."

"Tea, lovely." Aunt Kristina leaned out of the big chair,

clicking open her suitcase. "Erikka, a present for you, from Boston. I hope you like it." She took out something flat and wide, wrapped in a sweater.

It was a set of paints, bright liquid watercolors all the colors of jewels, in individual little bottles, like jars of medicine. And there was a block of paper, white as the sink.

"But you must show me how. I've never painted with paints like these," said Erikka shyly, touching the bottles of ultramarine, cyclamen, purple. "Would you? Show me?"

"Erikka, don't bother your aunt. She's had a long trip," called Mrs. Knorr over the kettle's hiss.

"Bring me a glass of water and I'll show you," said Aunt Kristina. "But what do you want a picture of?"

Erikka thought fast and reached for the shoebox of snapshots they kept in the bookcase. On the top was her favorite: a photograph of some hillside near where her second mother had grown up. Some place in New York State. "This," she said, thrusting the curling square at her aunt. And then she went to get the water.

"Thanks," said Aunt Kristina, dipping the brush quickly in and wetting the piece of paper.

"Erikka, come get your aunt's tea," called Mrs. Knorr.
"Oh, MOMMY!"

"Now. Or do you want to go to bed?"

Erikka raced into the kitchen. With irritating lethargy her mother was setting out some Girl Scout cookies on a plate. "Do you want a glass of milk?" asked her mother.

"No. Nothing."

"No, thank you."

"No, *thank you,* Mother dearest."

Mrs. Knorr couldn't help but smile. "Now, bring that tray inside. I'll be right in."

The tray was deposited with a crash on the coffee table, and Erikka dropped to the floor, open-mouthed.

Glistening, shiny like light on Lake Michigan, was a quick painting already. Just three or four areas of color, just several strokes—and there it was.

"You have to work fast, with watercolor, because it dries so quickly," said Aunt Kristina.

Erikka didn't say anything.

It was the loveliest thing she had ever seen; far, far more beautiful than anything in the Art Institute. It was more beautiful than anything in Chicago. Erikka reached out her hand to touch it.

"Don't, don't touch it," said Aunt Kristina. "It's not dry; you could easily mark it."

Erikka stared. The colors seemed to throb in it, as if they were parts of some live organism. Aunt Kristina had taken the color snapshot of a daylit mountainside and re-produced it in the secret colors of night: blues, and deeper blues, and up at the top midnight blues such as Erikka had never known about before. And then, that foreground of greens and blacks, all in sharp flowing shapes. And the best thing: at the top, the slender sliver of curling white. The very first night of a new moon.

"That's tonight's moon, the one I saw from the plane," said Aunt Kristina, reaching for her tea. "What do you think?"

"It's very nice," said Mrs. Knorr.

"Do another, so I can watch," Erikka begged.

"Erikka," warned Mrs. Knorr.

"Please?"

"Do you want to be sent to bed?" Mrs. Knorr wasn't kidding.

"Not till it's dry, so I can bring it with me," said Erikka.

"Some other time I'll demonstrate again," promised her aunt.

Inga and Annie were asleep. Erikka changed quickly into her nightgown, the comfortable white flannel one with rosebuds on it. She pushed Toby out into the hall and closed the bedroom door. Inga and Annie breathed hollow shushing sounds as they slept.

Erikka set her new picture up on the dresser, behind the candlestick from Mr. Tolyukov. Two treasures in one day! Two beautiful things to help combat the ugliness of the city around her! How strange that these two gifts should come on the same day.

With a sudden, suppressed giggle, she knew what she wanted to do. She reached in her bottom drawer, where she had hidden a book of matches and a white candle for just such an emergency, and then she lit the candle, and put it in the ornate old candlestick.

Now there were two tiny beacons of light in the darkened bedroom of the third-floor apartment on Merriam Street in the middle of Chicago, Illinois. Two little flashes of light: the steady small light of the candle, and behind it, the silvery light of the crescent moon.

And the two lights shone. Erikka stood at her dresser, unmindful of the fact that her mother might walk in at any minute. She stared entranced at the two lights, a pair of shining eyes almost, except that the moon, being new, was less bright.

Two shining eyes. In her amazement, and in her tiredness, Erikka forgot what her aunt had told her about not touching the picture. She reached forward, eager to feel the cool pine boughs in the foreground, eager to feel the soft wind that must be making those pines sway so.

Her eyes only on the two shining eyes in front of her, Erikka leaned forward, leaned her face into the branches of pine needles, leaned her arms into the cool of the mountain night air, leaned, leaned herself into the picture her aunt had painted for her.

Chapter Three

THE NIGHT
MOUNTAIN

It was almost like pushing through a curtain of sand. For a minute there was some inexplicable weight and density to the air around her; then, without warning, it stopped, and she was through.

Through! Through the painting—into it!

Could she have fallen asleep standing up at the dresser? Maybe it was a dream. But no, heavy in her hands, cold and intricate, was the candlestick. She must have lifted it, carried it through the painting—or maybe it had carried her. Maybe it was the magic thing, the key, the device by which she came. The flame still burned. It shed little light in the shadows of the pine trees.

The pine trees, the rustling wind, the grasses and sweeping shadows, the whole grand panorama of blue and green and midnight, it all stunned Erikka. She stood still for a moment, irresolute, reaching out a hand to touch a bough of pine needles, savoring its scratchiness.

She put down the candlestick carefully, right near the place she had come through.

And then she started walking.

There was more to the world, there was a lot more than just what had been in the painting. There was a sky much higher, with a sprawling display of stars; there was a kind of valley below, in which the still waters of a lake shone with reflected moonlight. There was a chill, a bite to the air; it was filled with the rich scent of things rotting and growing and changing; the scent of things living, Erikka thought.

She moved to an open space, keeping careful watch on the candle so as not to lose her way in the night forest. It was a cliffside, and the lake below glistened the color of plums.

Erikka began to move freely; she began to jump and stretch; it seemed as if she had to learn some new way to be, in order to fully appreciate this new place. Around the edge of the cliff she moved, slowly at first, making arches and circles with her hands. Then she moved more quickly, and lifted her legs, and jumped in the air. What was it here that made her want to dance?

I am alone, I am alone in my own world! she sang inside, and then she sang it outside: "I am alone, alone, alone in my own world!"

The moon shed little light.

The stars gave no warning.

An old woman stared at her.

A scream started in her, soared, shriveled; Erikka saw the shape of a woman in the pine trees, and then she fell to the ground in a dead faint.

* * *

"You wake up, you open the eyes," said a voice. "Oh, you wake up now, yes? Yes, you do, I think you do."

She didn't open her eyes though, not yet. Erikka felt a hand on her forehead, a hand touching the bridge of her nose, resting its fingertips lightly on her closed eyelids. She was afraid to look; was it Aunt Kristina, or Mommy, come into her room and found her in a nightmare, or was it someone else? Was she really on a mountainside? She didn't feel strong enough to find out.

"You open the eyes," said this voice, said these fingers encouragingly. "Don't be afraid, daughter."

She opened her eyes, to the great endless night sky, to the hand of the old, old woman.

"You'll be the surprise of my heart tonight, daughter," said the old woman. "Now do wake up, and tell me your name."

Erikka pulled herself up. And she didn't know why but she pulled away from the old woman and wrapped her arms around herself.

"Do I startle you, then?"

Erikka nodded, looking off into the shadows.

"Well, that's easily explained. But don't you want to come back to my rooms and I make you some tea?"

Erikka shook her head. She did not want to leave the candle; she also did not want to mention it, in case the old woman should steal it. She didn't feel that the old woman was a thief, but it seemed smartest to be on the safe side.

"Well, then, let's go sit and look at the lake, and you

tell me who you are and how you came here."

"Where are we?" asked Erikka.

"This is the mountain, of course. And this below us is the lake. Where do you live, daughter? In the town?"

"Far away," said Erikka. They walked over to a boulder at the side of the cliff and sat down. Erikka kept her arms around herself and her eyes on the indistinct distance.

"Well now, who are you?" The old woman picked up a twig and began prying caked mud out of the treads of her walking shoes.

"No, tell me who you are," said Erikka.

"My dear, I am Theresa Maloy, of the back hill. And I come out on this warm night because I feel there is something for me to see. Because I am lonely. And I see you dancing in the clearing, and you fall to the ground. And then I wake you up."

Erikka didn't know what to say. She clasped her knees through her flannel nightgown—here in the woods she was wearing slippers and a nightgown!—and thought. She'd read enough to know this might be anyplace at all, in the world or out of it. Probably out of it. Or that it could be a dream. It seemed real enough, though, with the winds rolling lengths of cloud past the moon, with the funny old woman staring at her.

My own private world, thought Erikka suddenly. A gift. A blessing. A world all alone, away from the Three Terrors and her mother and the Merriam Street merchants. She made a wish suddenly, to see if it was a magic world. She wished the old woman would disappear.

"Well?" said the old woman, not obliging.

"What are you doing out at night?" Erikka couldn't think of anything else to say, and she was disappointed her wish hadn't come true.

"When you get old you sometimes sleep poorly," said Theresa Maloy. "I walk at night when I cannot sleep."

Erikka was tired, puzzled, cold, and she might just as well say it. "Are you a witch?"

"And the little girl must ask this, too! Do I look like a witch?"

"Yes."

The old woman grunted and pulled her shawl around her tighter. It made her seem gaunt and poor. Her eyes were like pieces of highly polished mahogany; they caught the light and sent it flashing off. In her nickel-colored hair a comb of simple design lay like a hand, holding her straggling hairs in place. And her skirt was like her shawl: rough woven and dark. Her tough mountain boots (a large size) were laced with brown twine.

"I am a little less than a witch," said Theresa Maloy.

"But you said you were lonely, and then I came. Did you put on a spell to bring me here?"

"If loneliness is a spell to move people, then mine would be the strongest," said the old woman darkly. "But that is not the way of this world. I did not move you here."

She stared out over the lake, rubbing her knobby hands together. "At least, I don't think I did," she said.

"Wouldn't it be something if I did!" she said a little later. "Not that I could ever do it again."

Desire to be alone bubbled up in Erikka. "Don't you have to go home now?" she said, a little embarrassed but desperate.

"Oh, no," said Theresa happily. "I can't leave you alone. I don't even know your name or circumstance."

"Erikka."

"Ah, Erikka! Such a nice name, for one so young and lovely," said Theresa. "And do you live in this town?"

Something made Erikka want to keep silent about how she had arrived on this midnight mountainside. She could not tell what it was; Theresa seemed perfectly harmless. But there was some fear in Erikka, some reticence, and once again she bypassed the question.

"What is this town? I don't see it." She peered out over the valley.

"It is Canaan Lake," said Theresa, "of course. Are you not from the little village of Canaan Lake?"

Erikka's teeth clenched, ground. "No," she said. The whole world seemed suddenly telescoped, crowded, crammed together. This was Canaan Lake. This wasn't some other world, some magic kingdom. This was the actual spot in New York State that the photograph had been taken of and that Aunt Kristina had painted. This hill was jammed up right against her bedroom in Chicago somehow. It wasn't magic. It was real, disappointingly real. No wonder her wish hadn't worked.

"You're not a witch," said Erikka miserably. "You're just an old woman hobbling around on some regular hill."

"I don't say otherwise," said Theresa. But she sounded hurt.

"Phooey," said Erikka. "I'm going home."

Erikka covered her eyes and blinked hard. The old woman was puzzled; she stroked Erikka's long hair and murmured words that Erikka couldn't understand. "Are you lost, my dear, my daughter? Come home with me, I will help you find your home. Come now, my dear, I know what it is to be lost and alone; the very stars seem to ask why, from their high place; but you are not alone, my dear, my heart. Still your tears."

Erikka fingered the tears from her lashes.

"Come to my home on the back hill, I make you a cup of tea and build the fire to warm you," said Theresa. "Walking in the woods at night is wonderful, but sitting on a damp stone in a nightgown will bring a chill. And my bones are old; we go to my little house, and we think of what to do for you."

"No," said Erikka.

It was crazy, but she could only think of the number of times a poor unsuspecting child had been lured to a grisly death by a witch. There was Hansel and Gretel, the classic kidnapping case . . .

"Oh, my own, my love, you can't stay here and be damp and cold," cried Theresa. "Come out of the night; at home I have broth and bread. A nice fire, a blanket for your shoulders; and I give you money, if it is money you need to get home—"

"No," said Erikka again. "I'm going home." She stood up and moved a bit. A wind had just stirred from the lake, and vapors were rising in smoke-like spirals. She thought suddenly of the candle; she wanted to go back to it.

"Don't leave, daughter," said Theresa, in a voice of strange anguish. She rose and reached a knobby hand out.

The girl wrenched away and ran across the clearing. The winds had lifted from the lake and were starting to brush through the pine boughs around the clearing. Across the open space, the candle still burned in its ornate holder, set on the rock at the edge of the clearing.

"Don't run, you lose yourself in the woods! Erikka, come back!" Theresa started across the clearing in a loping, off-balance stride.

Erikka and the wind reached the candlestick at the same time. She had just clasped her right hand around the heavy base when the new wind blew out the flame; along the edge of the wind was etched the last worried word of Theresa: "No!"

The air again grew thick and heavy, and Erikka fell forward through it, through branches and colors and density, out into the bedroom, into her room in Chicago, Illinois, where Inga and Annie still lay sleeping. The candle had blown out.

She had to look at the picture again, but she didn't dare to light the candle. And if she turned on the bedroom light, she might wake up her sisters. So she carried the painting to the bedroom door.

All the lights in the house were off. Her mother and aunt must have gone to bed.

She flicked on the ugly fluorescent light above the medicine cabinet in the bathroom and studied the painting.

Nothing had changed. There was no trace of Theresa, no matter how hard she looked in the shadows. There was only the clearing, and the pine trees, and the slender moon.

And then Erikka, tired, crawled over Annie and Inga, to reach her own bed.

In the morning, there was the usual commotion that occurred while the children had their breakfast and got ready for school; the fact that Aunt Kristina was here made everything doubly complicated.

"Will you tell me what you think about that painting you gave me last night?" Erikka asked at the breakfast table.

"Eat that toast, Erikka, don't leave it there," said Mrs. Knorr. "More coffee, Kristina?"

"I want to be an artist, too," said Inga, kicking her legs against the wall as she ate. "Is it hard to be an artist, Aunt Kristina?"

"Stop kicking the wall or you'll wash those marks off it, Inga. Annie, darling, drink your juice."

"I don't WANT any juice," said Annie. She was a monster in the morning.

"It's hard to be an artist, but not impossible," said Aunt

Kristina. "Like anything else, it takes a lot of time and concentration."

"I drew a picture of a squirrel in Art last week," said Inga, "but Carmela Lopez took it to figure out her math average on the back of it."

"That painting, Aunt Kristina?"

"What about it, Erikka?" Kristina turned and looked at her.

She didn't know what she wanted to say. "What . . . what . . ."

"I don't WANT ANY JUICE!" screamed Annie, and in her fury she spilled the juice all over herself.

"Now look what you've done!" Mrs. Knorr wrested the empty glass out of Annie's clenched fist. "Here, Erikka, would you finish feeding Bengt while I wipe up this child?"

Erikka concentrated on getting the spoon into Bengt's mouth. "What would you name that painting?" It was a lame question, but it was all she could think of.

"That's just a sketch, a quick study. I made it be night because I like the moon." Aunt Kristina beamed at Bengt, who suffered an attack of shyness and tried to hide in his breakfast mush. "I ought to have painted you in it. The daughter of the moon, Erikka Knorr."

"Is that the thing on your dresser?" asked Inga.

"It's not a thing, it's a painting," said Erikka hotly.

"Well, it's nice," said Inga.

"Aunt Kristina did it."

"If you don't like it, Erikka, just toss it out. It's only a quick sketch. I won't be offended."

"Oh, no! I think it is positively beautiful! I wouldn't trade it for the world, Aunt Kristina." She turned and smiled. "I think you must be a wonderful person, to have painted that."

"You'll be late, Erikka, if you don't hurry," said Inga. "Can I wear your blue sweater today?"

"Oh, Inga, it's so big on you, it hangs down to your fingers."

"I roll it up. You can borrow my gray one if you want."

"You know I can't fit into your clothes. Go ahead, I'll even up the score some other time." Erikka pushed the rest of the food into Bengt's mouth quickly, as Inga gave Aunt Kristina a kiss. "See you at three o'clock!" Inga called as she ran down the stairs.

Inga was gone, Annie was in the bathroom being washed by Mrs. Knorr, and Bengt was too small to understand; now was the time. Erikka turned to her aunt.

"Is there anything funny about your painting?" she asked.

Aunt Kristina put her coffee cup down and leaned across the table so she could look carefully at her oldest niece. "What do you mean, Erikka? Does the painting upset you? Truthfully, I don't mind if you'd rather have something else . . ."

"No, I love it, Aunt Kristina." The girl felt desperate. She couldn't come right out and tell her aunt what had happened, but how else could she find out? "It's just—it's just that it affects me in a very strange way," she said slowly. "It feels almost magical."

Aunt Kristina reached out and took her hand. "Well, Erikka, that is a profoundly moving compliment you have paid to me, as an artist, but somehow I don't think I know what you mean. Suppose you think about it and talk to me later."

She stood up and lifted Bengt from the high chair. "I'll be here when you get home from school, I think; I don't plan on going out until this evening."

Erikka didn't know what to say.

"Erikka. Are you still here? You'll be late today for sure. Grab your books and your lunch and get going," said Mrs. Knorr, coming into the kitchen.

Erikka reached for her things and swung across the kitchen to give her aunt a kiss, and then flew out the door, leaving Aunt Kristina and her mother looking at each other and Bengt dribbling breakfast.

Chapter Four

A USELESS
MIRACLE

Tuesday afternoons at St. Mary's were always hopeless.

Erikka would start out with such enthusiasm. She would grip her pencil and lean over the paper and hum to herself, certain that today was going to be THE DAY. Today she was going to draw a picture worthy of universal admiration. The class would gasp! The eager, nervous young man who came once a week to teach Art would rush down the aisle and congratulate her. Even Sister Xaviera, stern and steady as a battleship, watching to be sure that things didn't get too out of hand, would take a few steps from the back of the room and nod approval.

Once, several years ago, Erikka had seen a beautiful print, a copy of some famous painting. It hung in Doreen O'Donald's living room, where Doreen had watched TV for years without noticing it. It was an outdoor restaurant, a café at the side of a river, and grownups were there in bright clothes, laughing and eating. One pretty lady was picking up a dog and talking to it.

Erikka had stood on the coffee table to get a better look. Doreen had said it was just like adults, having a good time and not inviting the kids. Mrs. O'Donald had yelled at Erikka for scratching the coffee table. And Erikka had decided she wanted to be an artist.

So, today being Tuesday, Erikka grew faint with hope that this would be the day she could finally draw. The young man passed out paper and crayons, and turned on the radio for atmosphere. Sister Xaviera, in the back of the room, rolled her eyes. The young man talked about tones and values and hues. Nobody listened. Erikka was trying to draw a picture of the night mountain. The old woman, Theresa, was hard to do, and she took up most of the page. The moon, up in a corner, looked like a banana on her head.

"Want to go get a soda after school?" whispered Doreen.

"No, thanks. I have to go to the bookstore," answered Erikka.

"Misses O'Donald and Knorr," boomed out Sister Xaviera warningly.

"Why, a picture of a—of a—" stammered the Art teacher, clutching Erikka's paper and turning it all ways. "Excellent lines. Keep up the good work." He thrust it back on her desk. The music blared on, tinny and thin and punctuated with a droning beat. Erikka sighed. Tuesdays were hopeless.

When Erikka arrived at the bookstore, Mr. Tolyukov was taking an order over the phone; he nodded and gave

Erikka a distracted wave. There were no other customers just now. With a feeling of doom, Erikka wondered if Mrs. Pruitt had sent a new check, or come back and signed the old one. She reached down and picked up the Countess, who was sleeping in the window display again, next to some new dictionaries. The black cat didn't resist at all, and Erikka lavished motherly attention on her. After a while Mr. Tolyukov hung up the phone, and the Countess jumped out of Erikka's arms and back to her place among the dictionaries.

"Good day, my young friend," said Tolyukov.

"Hello. Did you call Mrs. Pruitt last night?"

"Ah, that's business, my little one. Why don't we skip business today and think of more pleasant things?"

"It might be business, but it's *my* business, Mr. Tolyukov. Please. Tell me what happened."

"Why don't you make some tea, and then we'll talk," said Tolyukov.

Erikka hurried to the back room. Once again she went through the ritual of setting the kettle on to boil and arranging the teacups on the tray with the mysterious domes of the Cathedral of St. Basil. And again, she envied Tolyukov his little isolated island of a home, with everything just in its place and no screaming brothers or sisters at war under his feet. On the counter was the precious blue vase that Erikka had left in his safekeeping. Precious things, thought Erikka: a blue vase that was my first mother's, a picture painted by my aunt, a candlestick loaned by a friend. I want to surround myself with wonderful things.

She carried the tray to the front room. Mr. Tolyukov was waiting on an elderly lady.

"And is this your little helper?" asked the old lady, giving Erikka a smile.

Erikka nodded quickly. Some help she had been!

When the lady was gone, Tolyukov turned and picked up his cup of tea. "Where's your friend? The curly-headed one?"

"He's busy with chores." Erikka climbed up on the stool behind the counter. "Tell me something about your home. Tell me about the Countess."

"I guess you mean the first Countess, not my lovely feline companion," said Tolyukov seriously.

"Yes, the one you were in love with. Countess Olga."

"Countess Olga Molokiev. The daughter of a very wealthy landowner. You've heard all about her, Erikka; I've told you how we met, how we fell in love, how I came to America, and how she was supposed to follow; and how we lost contact with each other during the war, and how, when I went back to Russia ten years ago to look for her, no one had seen or heard from her for years. Why do you want to hear such a sad story, Erikka? Do you imagine that it is only a story? You know it is true; terrible things can happen as well as wonderful things in this world. Why do you want to hear that?"

Erikka felt awful. "I thought you liked to talk about the Countess. I wanted to cheer you up."

Tolyukov looked at her. "Well, you are right," he said at last. "Talking about something is the only consolation at times. It is a small one, but it *is* consolation. I will tell you again what she looked like when I met her."

Erikka swirled the tea in her cup and studied the waves.

"I had come to the big house as a tutor; you know that her father was rich, and he had his children taught right at home, as was the fashion in those days among the wealthy. I came to live in the house, to teach three children their letters and logic and composition. When I took the position, I thought that the children were very young. But on the day I arrived, the door was opened by a lovely young woman."

"The Countess," said Erikka, because she knew this story well.

"I said to her, 'I am Modest Mikhailovich Tolyukov, come to teach the children.' She bowed and said, 'And I am the oldest child, Olga.'

"Erikka, she was the loveliest thing I had ever seen. Now I am an old man, surrounded by books and dust and the noise of a big American city, but in all those years between the time I first saw Olga and right now, with you at my side, I have never seen a person more splendid."

Erikka stared. She loved this story.

"She was dressed in a long, flowing skirt, cream-colored, with black stitching, and she carried a black parasol and a pair of gloves in her hand. Her hair was swept up on top of her head in the fashion of the day, like a loaf of bread, perfectly formed, remarkable. Somehow the sun was shining on the marble floor behind her, and the light swam up around her, Erikka: a sight to remember."

"Did you go right inside? Did she show you to your room?"

"I went inside, and the stout lady who managed all the servants came to greet me. She sent Olga on her way; her father was taking her out riding for the afternoon. Olga paused at the door and looked at me, and although it was the fashion of the day for a young woman to be coy and flirtatious, Olga Molokiev would not stoop to such nonsense. She looked me straight in the eye and smiled, and it was as serious and purposeful a smile as I have ever seen on the face of any woman or man since."

"Was she in love with you from the start?"

Tolyukov laughed. "You have only my word for it, Erikka, but yes, she was. We had planned to be married soon, but Russia was up in arms for the war—the First World War, I'm talking about. The Revolution swept in, and we made plans to leave. We were talking about marriage the day we got that old candlestick. But Olga wanted to go home to visit her family one final time—she'd been working as a nurse in the army—and we parted. We agreed I would go on ahead to America and she would follow as soon after as she could. But with the country in turmoil and being a half a world apart, somehow we lost touch. I wrote constantly to her family but never received a word in return. Perhaps she made it to Europe, perhaps she never left her family.

"I moved from New York to Chicago, and left forwarding addresses everywhere, but as the years passed it became evident that we had lost the crucial contact with each other. All she had was the one address of my first room in Brooklyn, and that was many, many years ago. Even if she did come over and look for me there, she could not find me. And so, I am left with a wonderful memory that has lasted me all my life through."

"But it's so sad," Erikka said, sniffing.

"Not so sad, Erikka. Many a man or woman has spent a lifetime with less than that. A single love, true, but experienced with pride. A lifetime could be wasted doing worse."

This was terrible. Erikka was supposed to be cheering him up; instead, he was making her cry.

"Maybe she'll come yet," she said.

"Yes, maybe," said Tolyukov warmly. "In the meantime, and while we wait, would you like some more tea?"

"No. Mr. Tolyukov, tell me what happened when you talked to Mrs. Pruitt last night."

"Are you determined to hear?" he asked her. The door opened and a couple of customers came in.

"Yes, please," she said.

"She's returning today to sign that check. She sounded annoyed. But we have been doing business together for several years now, and she trusts me to sell her the best books I can get. Without the Pruitts' business, I'd have a hard time making ends meet. They're very steady and important customers. So you mustn't judge them too harshly, Erikka."

Tolyukov turned to make a sale. Erikka took the teacups and tray into the back room and started running hot water into the sink. While it was filling, she turned and looked around. The bed, the table and chairs, the chest with the nice painting on it, the closet, the shoes in a neat row under the bed. It was all that Mr. Tolyukov had, since he didn't have his Countess and he never would.

And though it was so neat and perfect, for the first time Erikka noticed that the wall above the sink was crumbling. It needed plastering and painting. Maybe Tolyukov didn't have enough money to get it repaired.

She looked at the blue vase that had belonged to her first mother. Maybe she could bring some spring flowers, now that it was April. Maybe some daffodils; they would look nice in that vase and would help cheer Mr. Tolyukov up.

Thinking about the blue vase reminded Erikka about the candlestick that Tolyukov had loaned to her in exchange; and then the trembling memory of last night came back to her. She finished washing the teacups and set them back in their places in the cabinet, and returned to the front room.

The old man was gift-wrapping a couple of books for a customer. Erikka pulled out the ribbon when he was ready for it. He smiled at her and said, "You are my good friend, Erikka."

"Do you believe in miracles, Mr. Tolyukov?" Erikka asked when the customer had left. She was thinking of last night.

"Of course, I do," he said.

"Like angels, and stuff?"

"All sorts of miracles. I would be startled at nothing. If the exalted President himself were to walk in here and ask for a book of poetry, I would only say, 'Mr. President, may I recommend this slender volume by Tennyson?' And all the President's bodyguards would say, 'This is the President! You ought to be thrilled speechless!' And I would say, 'But, gentlemen, it does not surprise me that the President of the United States would enjoy reading a volume of poetry.' Of course, I would pick out a thin book, because I know he does not have much extra time to read for enjoyment."

"What would be a miracle for you?" he asked Erikka.

She had forgotten all about why she had asked him in the first place. "To have a place for myself. All alone, without anyone else." Erikka spoke without hesitation.

Mr. Tolyukov was not listening. "Odd that you should bring up the subject," he said. "Just today I took out from its place a second edition of a volume of poetry by Walt Whitman, your famous American poet, and I read a few lines . . . let's see if I can find them . . ." He fingered through the pages.

"What's a second edition?" asked Erikka.

"Hmmm? Oh, a first edition means a first printing. When a book is published, you see, a certain amount of copies are printed, say, a thousand. These thousand may have the words 'First Printing' in them. When they are all sold, if there is still a market for the book, then the publisher might print another thousand. This would be the second printing. If a book is really popular, it might go through a lot of printings. This book did. Whitman kept changing it each time, adding and rearranging his poems, so all the early printings differ slightly. Every time a printing incorporates some changes in the text, it is a new edition. All the early editions of Whitman's poems are quite valuable."

"And you have a second edition? Of Whitman's poetry?"

"Yes. The 1856 edition of *Leaves of Grass*. Here, listen to these lines."

"But it might be a valuable book!"

" 'Why, who makes much of a miracle? As to me I know of nothing else but miracles—' " quoted Tolyukov with his funny, froggy smile.

"Don't you think it might be worth something? If it is so old?"

"Of course; and there is another reason. Come here and look."

Tolyukov flipped the book to the front. On the title page someone had written in an old, brown ink.

"What does it say?" asked Erikka, impatient.

"It says, 'Walt Whitman,' " Tolyukov told her proudly.

Erikka almost fell off her stool. "Is this an autographed book? By a famous poet who's dead? Mr. Tolyukov, is this worth something?"

"Not so loud, Erikka. Yes, it is worth something, quite a bit, I am told. It came into my hands accidentally a number of years ago; in fact, I didn't even know I had it for several years. It was in a box of old books I bought second-hand from the estate of some old woman who had died. And it is my prize possession. You talk about miracles; this is a miracle: that someone as poor as I could have come across such a treasure."

"But, Mr. Tolyukov!" Erikka was beside herself. "You could sell it. You could sell it for a lot of money, and have your walls plastered—"

"I don't want to sell it, Erikka," said Tolyukov gently.

"What a great thing to have! Do you have any more autographed Walt Whitman books?"

"Excuse me," said a voice that turned Erikka to ice. She whirled around.

Mrs. Pruitt glared. Her hard eyes bored into Erikka's. In one gloved hand she held a long white envelope, with which she kept hitting the palm of her other gloved hand.

"Good afternoon, Mrs. Pruitt," said Mr. Tolyukov.

For a well-bred lady, Mrs. Pruitt moved fast. Before anyone knew what had happened, she had leaned over the counter and grabbed the book that Tolyukov had been quoting out of. She flipped through to the front.

She stared at the first page.

"Have you had this authenticated?" Her voice was very low.

"Yes, ma'am, I have," said Tolyukov. Things had suddenly taken a very serious tone, or Erikka would have asked what authenticated meant.

"What are you asking for it?"

"I am not asking anything for it; it is not for sale."

Mrs. Pruitt turned pale. "Mr. Tolyukov! Our agreement. We do our rare-book dealing here in return for your loyal cooperation. You have promised us first refusal on any important find."

Tolyukov looked pained. "Mrs. Pruitt, were it for sale, you would be the first person it would be offered to. But I'm afraid it is not. I owned this long before I became your purchaser. I merely took it out to show my friend Erikka."

Still she held it. "But, Mr. Tolyukov, I want this volume for the library that my husband and I have been accumulating for many years. I will give you what the book is worth—and we're talking in five figures, you know. Our arrangement . . . our agreement . . ."

"I am very fortunate to have your business," said Tolyukov. "And I am exceedingly grateful. But the book is mine, Mrs. Pruitt. It belongs to my library of rare books, of which it is the sole volume."

Mrs. Pruitt's manner softened. "Mr. Tolyukov," she said, and her voice had changed its tone, "we certainly can see our way clear to some understanding? You can't possibly have the resources for the protection and preservation that this book deserves. You know we would give it a good home. Eventually our library will be left to some scholarly institution, where everyone will benefit. You must reconsider. It really would be our pleasure to pay you handsomely for this book. Please."

"You are making me feel very rude," said Tolyukov. "But I cannot say yes. I am very sorry."

Mrs. Pruitt almost looked as if she would cry momentarily. She stared at the book in her hand, and then at Erikka and Mr. Tolyukov. For a moment she seemed unsure what should come next.

Tolyukov reached out and gently took the book back.

As it slid out of her hand, her old spirit came back to her. "This is really an outrage, Mr. Tolyukov, and one that I am ashamed to witness. A fine, important book like that should not be left to rot in the hands of a second-hand bookseller who hasn't even the sense to have it housed in ideal conditions."

She tore up the envelope in small fluttering pieces.

"When you see fit to talk business, Mr. Tolyukov, then business will be conducted. And not until."

She stuffed the pieces of envelope in her purse and stormed out.

"She's in love with art, but she doesn't care about people," said Tolyukov wearily. "It's a sad thing."

"She ripped up her check," said Erikka. "Now what will you do?"

Tolyukov sat down on the stool and shook his head.

"Was it a *big* check? Do you really need that money?"

"Oh, Erikka Knorr," he said.

"Will you call her up? Call the police? Take her to court?"

Tolyukov leaned on the counter and entwined his fingers. "Maybe I should just consider closing down. After all, when you come right down to it, maybe this is an indication that I should just quit."

"You could fight her in court!" cried Erikka.

"What's the sense of pinching pennies, and robbing Peter to pay Paul, at my age? I've gone on and on in this old shop, and I'm not inclined to go out looking for new patrons and customers at my age. I'm too tired, and I'm probably too old."

"If you sold your book . . ." said Erikka quietly.

Tolyukov didn't look at her. "Oh, I don't expect you to understand. It is an old man's peculiarity, I know." He hummed for a minute, thinking. "I can't afford to run the store as a hobby, Erikka. Without a dependable steady customer to count on, I'd have to juggle pennies and worry and scrape. I could do it, but why should I? If I'm not making a profit, why should I go on? Besides, it's been years and years; I'm just too old to begin again from scratch. I belong to a different era, and I should remember that, I guess."

Erikka wanted to argue, to inflate old Tolyukov with ambition and determination. But suddenly he looked so dreadfully old and exhausted, and a lot of it was her fault. She hadn't meant to be trouble, but the Pruitts' not paying their bill was really because of her. And now Tolyukov talked tiredly of closing the shop. She couldn't stand it—but she could argue no more. Containing her impatience out of consideration for him, she remained unhappy and voiceless.

They sat in silence.

A minute later the door opened again. Neither of them looked up.

"What's so absorbing that you don't say hello?"

Then they did look up; it was Francisco de Medina, the young man from the Philippines who was studying to be a doctor and played the violin. He had his violin case with him.

"Oh, play, anything!" cried Erikka.

Francisco could see something was wrong. He opened his case on the counter, rosined his bow, spent a minute or two tuning the four strings, and then he began to play.

Erikka watched him. His eyes closed, his arm moved, his head was turned so as to take the instrument under his chin, his fingers moved, his foot tapped silently, and because of all this, the bookstore was filled with a fluid spirit, a spirit of something Erikka had a hard time naming. The music moved around them, like a mist, like a charm. The spirit of a miracle, Erikka thought. And that is what we need.

Francisco played and played and played.

Chapter Five

AN ATTEMPT AT
HARMONY

Determination was Erikka's new quality. She decided this on the way to school the next morning. She would be as firm as a rock, hard and stalwart as steel. Things were whirling around her as in a hurricane wind—wasn't Tolyukov being swept away from her? Not him, *too,* she said to herself heatedly. It's happened too often, I won't *allow* it to happen again. Tolyukov's age and discouragement had impressed on Erikka the need for strength. So she would be the constant hope, noble as the Statue of Liberty. And she would work miracles, like a saint. She would go to the Pruitts and ask for their charity in a resolute way. They would be astounded at her humility and determination. They would fall over themselves in apologies and retractions.

When school let out, Erikka gave her books to Inga and ran off toward the Dearborn School for Boys, just a few blocks away. Simon would have to come, too.

She stopped at a corner, toes in the street, heels on the curb. The policewoman directing traffic must be thinking what a fine, steadfast girl she was. "Curb, doll, or you'll lose them toes," sang out the policewoman.

The Dearborn School loomed up, crowding its proud pillars and tall windows almost out to the street. It always seemed to be swelling, those pilasters and porticos in dirty red stone and pairs of squat chimneys. Erikka ran up the stone steps and drew in a deep breath. The mammoth door must have been designed to be so large and heavy that only a grownup could open it. But Erikka got a grip on the iron handle, and heaved, and wheezed, and then slipped into the dark, high hall, which smelled of onions and chalk dust.

"May I help you?" asked the tight-lipped young man at the desk.

"I'm here to see Simon Cameron, fourth division," said Erikka. She always talked in a low voice when she came here. She was afraid if she spoke incorrectly or rudely, they might take her and lock her in an attic somewhere.

The man spoke into a telephone, and then directed Erikka to a waiting room.

When Simon arrived, Erikka jumped out of the cold fake-leather chair.

"Are you grounded for life?"

"For a week," said Simon. "But listen: the afternoon proctor's grandmother had a stroke and he had to go away suddenly, so I *could* sneak out and meet you on the corner in ten minutes. I'll just have to tell someone to alibi for me if anyone notices."

"Good." They hurried apart, Erikka past the receptionist, Simon fading back into the dark echoing corridors of the school. Erikka was careful to nod politely to the receptionist (she was practicing humility and tact). A while later, Erikka and Simon were running away from any eyes that might be peering from the tall dark windows.

There was no time for lengthy narrative. Erikka told Simon what had happened so far: that Mrs. Pruitt hadn't paid her bill; that Tolyukov had a copy of a book Mrs. Pruitt really wanted; that since it was partly their fault that she hadn't signed the check in the first place, they had an obligation to try to fix things up.

"But what are we to do?" he asked. "We can't blow Mrs. Pruitt up."

"This calls for even more drastic measures," said Erikka solemnly.

"More drastic than that?" Simon sounded astonished.

"Yes." Erikka paused for dramatic effect. "Simon, we are going to have to apologize."

Simon whistled. "So you think that would do some good?"

"It can't hurt," she said. "And maybe it'll be just the thing."

"All right," he said. "You're the boss."

They reached the Pulaski Drugstore. Erikka found a phone booth in the corner behind the greeting cards. She looked up the Pruitts' address. They lived in a high-rise apartment building on Lake Shore Drive.

"Call them," said Simon. He gave her a dime.

"Say a prayer," said Erikka as she dialed.

After the third ring a lady said, "Good afternoon, Hexler Pruitt residence, Judith Cooper speaking."

"May I speak to Mr. or Mrs. Pruitt?" said Erikka.

"Who's calling and is there a message?" said the voice.

"Well, I want to see Mr. and Mrs. Pruitt—this is Erikka Knorr."

"Is this of a business or personal nature, Miss Knorr?"

"Uh—uh—," groped Erikka. Then sudden inspiration. "Business," she said. "I'm calling about a volume of poetry Mrs. Pruitt is eager to buy."

There was a pause and the sound of pages flipping. "Mrs. Hexler Pruitt can see you this evening at seven o'clock," she said.

"Fine, I'll be there," Erikka agreed, and hung up.

"A volume of poetry Mrs. Pruitt is eager to buy?" Simon asked.

"That was just to get us in there," said Erikka. "We can explain ourselves once we're there. Now, the real problem: do you think you can sneak out tonight?"

"Usually it's impossible—but if the proctor's still off somewhere—"

"Simon!" Erikka's jaw dropped. "I can't go by myself!"

"I know, I know. I'll see what I can do. Meanwhile, we better head back to the prison. I'm in their bad graces enough as it is already without being caught now. Especially if I'm breaking out again tonight."

Erikka sighed. "You know what I'd like to do? Jump on

a bus and go down to the museum. Wouldn't it be nice to spend a peaceful afternoon there, looking at things?"

"I don't know," said Simon. "Depending on whether or not the school attendants were standing outside with ropes and nets waiting to catch me."

"Six-fifteen. I'll meet you at our regular corner," said Erikka. "Let's synchronize our watches."

"I haven't got one."

"Neither have I." They laughed.

At their regular corner they met, on time, Erikka fresh from the museum, where she'd looked in the museum shop for a present for Aunt Kristina, and Simon from his school.

Simon told Erikka he had pretended he was taking out the garbage. "The boys in my room won't squeal on me," he said. "But even so, the earlier we get back, the better."

They were silent on the elevated train. Each one was thinking of things to say to the Pruitts. At one stop, a man dressed just in a hospital gown lurched into their car. He had bare feet and an identification tag around one wrist. Everyone in the car stared out the windows fixedly, except Simon.

"Don't look at him, Simon, he might come over here, he might be a crazy man," hissed Erikka between clamped teeth, paying such intense attention to the city beneath them that she might have been expecting to find the Secret of Life somewhere down there in the alleys and gutters.

But Simon couldn't help it. He felt sorry for the man, who must have leaped up out of a hospital bed, and ducked nurses and doctors, and shot past the receptionist, and thrown himself through the doors into the street. That took some courage.

"Did I tell you, no, I didn't," said Erikka rapidly, "about the candle and the painting?" Simon looked at her and she poured the story out, to keep the crazy man from coming near them, perhaps, and saying something.

When Erikka had finished, Simon said, "Pretty good."

"It wasn't good or bad, it was just weird."

"I mean, as a story. You've changed your mind? You want to be a writer instead of an artist—"

"I don't want to be a writer," said Erikka, not comprehending, and then, "Oh. You think I'm making it up."

Simon looked surprised. "Should I have pretended to believe it?"

Erikka was furious for a minute, raging, whipping anger. But she suddenly recalled her new trait: ironbound staunchness. Or maybe it was obstinacy. Whatever its name, now would be a good time to display it.

"I'm sorry if you don't believe me," she said. "But it's true. Here's our stop." She smiled, peace invoked if not restored.

They had to squeeze past the runaway in the hospital gown to get off the el.

"You never know what you're going to find in this city," said Simon as they walked.

"It's a dangerous place! Crazy men like that running loose—"

"Ah, he wasn't doing any harm. He probably just wanted to go home," said Simon gently.

Erikka didn't answer.

There was a doorman, in brass and blue and piping, who let them in, and an elevator man in similar garb who pressed the right buttons and who pointed the way down the hall when they got out. The rugs were as thick as a lawn of summer grass. Everything was very very quiet.

"You do the talking," said Erikka suddenly, firmly, just as she knocked.

"Not on your life," said Simon out of the corner of his smile.

The door was opened by an enormous woman, whose body was so large and face so small that when she stood erect, her head was nearly impossible to see.

"No soliciting in this building!" she said, and closed the door.

"Soliciting?" asked Simon.

"I think it means trying to sell something."

"I'll sell her to the zoo!" Simon growled.

"Patience!" said Erikka. She knocked again.

The woman returned. She looked like a mammoth up-ended sofa, all buttons and upholstery. She did not appear pleased.

"We are not soliciting," said Erikka quickly.

"Go away," said the sofa, "or I'll call the police." The door began to close again.

"We have an appointment with Mrs. Pruitt," said Erikka loudly, right up to the woman's angry little face, which was contorting and swelling like a pastry in an oven.

The pastry deflated. "Oh," she said. "Miss Knorr?" The door opened wider.

"The same," said Erikka proudly.

"Won't you come in?" said the woman. "This way, please."

They followed her down a hall to a set of highly polished doors with gold-painted beveling. Inside was a living room with a fireplace and a wide window overlooking Lake Michigan.

"The Pruitts will be with you presently," said the woman. She left them there.

"I don't know what we're doing here," sang Simon very lightly.

"Brace yourself," replied Erikka.

The doors were swung open again by the sofa-lady. In sailed Mr. and Mrs. Pruitt.

"Judith—children?" said Mrs. Pruitt.

"Or so they appear," said the sofa-woman, who must have been Judith.

She doesn't recognize us, thought Erikka. Maybe to her, all children look alike.

"A little diversion, darling," said Mr. Pruitt.

"Judith, perhaps some sherry, it being that time of day," said Mrs. Pruitt.

"Right away," said Judith, and disappeared as gracefully and silently as a sofa is able to.

Mrs. and Mr. Pruitt sat in great chairs by the fire. Mr. Pruitt loosened his belt a notch. Mrs. Pruitt arranged the folds of her dress to fall neatly over the edge of the chair. Then they turned to the children.

"Such a novelty, having children here!" said Mrs. Pruitt, with a smile. "To whom or what do we owe our gratitude for your visit?"

Neither Simon nor Erikka was sure of that, so they just smiled back at her.

Mr. and Mrs. Pruitt smiled.

"Your names?" said Mr. Pruitt, after a time.

"Oh," said Simon. "I'm Simon Cameron."

"And I'm Erikka Knorr."

"And I'm simply breathless for that sherry," said Mrs. Pruitt wittily. She rang a little bell that stood on the table next to her chair.

Judith arrived with the sherry. Mr. Pruitt snatched a glass off the tray and said, "To your health, Regina," and took a taste. Mrs. Pruitt placed hers, untouched, on a table beside her.

"Now. Down to business. What can we help you with?"

Erikka took a deep breath.

"You see," she said, "we are the two people who were in Mr. Tolyukov's bookstore a couple of days ago, the day the Countess scratched you and you threw the book at her and walked out without paying. Since it was partly our fault, all that confusion and trouble, we decided to come here and apologize. We don't want Mr. Tolyukov to have to lose his store. We are sorry for the commotion. It was our fault, all our fault."

"Yes," said Simon.

Mrs. Pruitt looked at Mr. Pruitt. "Lose his store?" she said in a delicate voice. "Why should he do that?"

"He's not *rich,* you know," said Erikka. "He needs your business. He has to pay bills. Even the wall near his sink needs plastering."

"Well," said Mr. Pruitt, "if you have poor business practices, naturally your business is going to suffer. A shame."

"Your business will *fail* if you operate it unscrupulously," said Mrs. Pruitt.

Erikka felt as if things were getting away from the point. "So we're very sorry," she said loudly. "Everything was our fault."

Mrs. Pruitt looked at Mr. Pruitt. She took a sip of sherry and then said, "Browler, is this that special sherry we ordered from Spain last year?"

"Yes," said Mr. Pruitt.

"Delightful. Now, where were we?"

"We had just apologized," said Simon.

"Oh, yes. Charming of you, really; don't you agree, Browler? Of course, there is no excuse for rude shenanigans such as we were all the unfortunate witnesses of that afternoon—but boys will be boys."

"And girls, girls," said Browler, with a smile for Erikka.

And idiots, idiots, thought Erikka, smiling back.

"Now," said Mrs. Pruitt, putting down her glass and fixing her stare on Erikka, "you have shown yourself to be, if not *good* children, at least capable of improvement. I appreciate your apologies."

"Will you change your mind about signing the check?" asked Erikka.

"Please?" said Simon.

"It's a problem, truly," said Mrs. Pruitt. "Now, where is that Judith?" She shook the little brass bell.

Judith appeared, breathless.

"Did you take the phone call from Miss Knorr earlier today, Judith?" Mrs. Pruitt asked her.

"Yes, ma'am, I did," said Judith.

"And the nature of the business to be discussed?"

"A volume of poetry," said Judith, "for sale."

"That," said Mrs. Pruitt, "is why I have chosen to see you."

"But I don't know anything about any books of poetry," said Erikka. "I'm afraid I only said that to get your attention."

"You have it," said Mrs. Pruitt.

"Will there be anything else?" asked Judith.

"No," said Mr. Pruitt. Judith left. Mr. Pruitt leaned forward in his chair.

"You are a good friend of Modest Tolyukov," said Mr. Pruitt.

"Yes," said Erikka faintly.

"And you don't wish to see him close down his business."

"No."

"Well, then," said Mr. Pruitt with a tremendous smile.

"Well said!" Mrs. Pruitt applauded with enthusiasm.

Erikka glanced at Simon. I don't get it, her glance said. They're thoroughly mad, suggested Simon's return glance.

"What do you think?" asked Mr. Pruitt.

"I think it's scintillating," said Mrs. Pruitt.

"Not you, Regina; I'm talking to the children."

"Well," said Erikka, "I don't think I understand."

"Sweet child, it's simple," said Regina Hexler Pruitt. She reached out and took Erikka's hand in hers. "Your youthful innocent charm is powerful enough to sway Mr. Tolyukov. You must convince him to part with that volume of poetry that I saw in his hands the other afternoon. The one with Walt Whitman's own signature in the front. You can do it, you are loyal, a true friend. Convince him, and we'll pay our bill at once. Not only that, I'll pay him handsomely for that book."

"*Very* handsomely, I might add," said Mr. Pruitt.

"What do you say?" asked Mrs. Pruitt.

Erikka felt trapped. She looked at Simon, who had pushed himself back in his chair as far as he could go, as if he were in danger of being contaminated by the velvety persuasions of the Pruitts. His eyes glowed like light on water.

"I think it's a good idea," Erikka said slowly.

"Of course it is!" chorused the Pruitts. Simon simply stared.

"But I already tried it," she admitted. "I already had that idea, Mrs. Pruitt. I don't know why he wants to hang on to that book. But he does. It's important to him. He won't part with it for anything."

The overwhelming joy in Mrs. Pruitt's smile subsided, leaving it looking slightly mechanical.

"But, dearest," she said, "how hard could you have tried?"

"My hardest," Erikka confessed.

"Try HARDER," suggested Mrs. Pruitt, in a voice like a cannon.

"Okay," said Erikka.

"Look here, kids," said Mr. Pruitt. "Let's be reasonable."

"Yes, let's be reasonable," said Mrs. Pruitt. "It's a matter of business ethics, after all. We have had a long-standing agreement with Mr. Tolyukov for first refusal on any item of special note. His holding back on this book is unprofessional and disappointing. We have patronized his little establishment for years. This is ingratitude of the first order."

"You must realize, kids, that Regina is most interested in volumes of poetry," said Mr. Pruitt, wiping his brow with a handkerchief. "She has an impressive collection of rare books."

Mrs. Pruitt nodded, modest but honest. "Only the best."

"And since she has such an interest, such a consuming

passion for things artistic, and since she would take such excellent care of such a volume, much better care than our friend Tolyukov could ever afford, then she has a *right* to that volume!" concluded Browler Pruitt.

"A moral right," said Mrs. Pruitt. "A God-given sacred duty."

Mr. Pruitt took out his wallet. "Let's make this a business deal," he said. "Fifty dollars now, and an additional two hundred when you persuade Mr. Tolyukov to sell us that book."

"An appetizer now, a feast to follow!" said Mrs. Pruitt.

"That's two hundred and fifty dollars," said Mr. Pruitt, "above and beyond the considerable figure I intend to pay Mr. Tolyukov for the volume itself."

"Think of all the lovely ice cream! Think of the candy you could buy for two hundred and fifty dollars," said Mrs. Pruitt, taking another sip.

"Think of the joy you would bring to a poor woman's heart," said Mr. Pruitt. Mrs. Pruitt cast her eyes on the imported Persian carpet on the inlaid floor and looked properly grateful and humble.

"Think of your part in helping old Tolyukov retain his little bookstore," said Browler Pruitt.

"Think!" ordered Regina Pruitt from her position of gratitude.

Erikka glanced at Simon again. He looked as if he might, any minute, pitch himself through the windows, just to get away from this.

"No," said Erikka.

Browler Pruitt's jaw dropped and his pipe fell to the carpet, where it burned a little black spot.

Regina Pruitt straightened up her back and gripped the arms of her chair. "Have we been too stern with you?"

"Oh, no," said Erikka.

"Browler and I never had children. So you see, we've never learned how to behave with them. You must tell us how we've done."

"Admirably," said Erikka. Simon just rolled his eyes.

"What would you *like* us to offer you in return for your getting Tolyukov to sell us that book?"

"Nothing," said Simon. "Nothing." He put his feet on the floor. "Erikka has told you, Mr. Tolyukov doesn't want to sell it. So he's not going to. Now we came to apologize for the commotion in the store the other day, and we apologized. I think we ought to go home."

"What!" said Mrs. Pruitt. "Why, the impertinence of you—"

"He's not," said Erikka hotly. "He's right. We don't want your two hundred and fifty dollars. We can't persuade Mr. Tolyukov to sell you that book. All we wanted to do—"

"We've done," finished Simon. "So come on, Erikka, let's get out of here."

"More sherry, ma'am?" asked Judith, coming in. "Or do you want me to just leave the bottle with you?"

"Don't be rash," said Mrs. Pruitt. "Browler, do something."

"Goodbye," said Erikka.

"You're being rash!" said Mrs. Pruitt.

"All I can say—" said Browler Pruitt, but nobody listened.

"Shall I show the guests to the door?" asked Judith Cooper brightly. She suddenly seemed to be enjoying herself immensely.

"I shall get that book," said Regina Hexler Pruitt. She raised a finger to heaven. "Mark my words."

Simon pushed open the door, and he and Erikka ran out.

"They don't seem to be marking your words, dear," Mr. Pruitt was saying.

Judith Cooper had followed them. "You're not bad kids," she grunted approvingly. "I don't think I've ever seen them in such a state." She unlocked the entrance door and opened it for them. "Don't take it too hard," she said, winking.

Erikka and Simon raced to the elevators.

After they had stopped laughing, things seemed worse than ever. "We meant to be *pleasant*," said Erikka in dismay. "How could it have gone so wrong? All we've done is make them angrier and angrier."

The train screamed into the station, and they boarded it.

"We tried," said Simon.

"Well, we failed, too!" said Erikka. "We seem destined to just ruin things for Tolyukov."

"They're already ruined," said Simon. "They can't get any worse."

"I wonder." Erikka put her head in her hands and

looked out the window, at the alleys and fire escapes and garbage cans and trash. "Maybe I'll go back to the night mountain tonight," she said, almost to herself.

"Don't start that again," Simon said.

She just kept looking out the window.

Chapter Six

THE NIGHT MOUNTAIN AGAIN

W hen Erikka passed the Merriam Deli, she tapped on the glass and waved. Florry was carting a huge ham to the slicer. She set it down, and then dramatically drew a finger across her neck, making a horrible face at Erikka. The bearded gentleman waiting at the counter was mystified, but Erikka knew what she meant. Trouble.

She unlocked the door to the apartment and ran upstairs.

Mrs. Knorr was standing at the top of the steps with her arms folded.

"I want to know where you have been till nine o'clock at night," said her mother.

"I was with my friend Simon," said Erikka, standing on the stairs.

"Till nine o'clock? What is the meaning of this? Who is this Simon, anyway? Who do you think you are, running around Chicago all night? Do you know I called your father's dispatcher and told them to call him and have him come right home?" Her voice rose in pitch and volume, and although Erikka wouldn't look at her face, she could see the edges of her mother's apron wavering; Mrs. Knorr must be shaking with anger.

"Do you know where your Aunt Kristina is now? She's out on foot, combing the neighborhood. Do you know that you are four hours late for supper? Answer me, young woman!"

"I thought tonight was your teaching night," said Erikka.

"Oh, you did? And you run about the town like a wild animal when I'm not here? Get up here, take off that coat."

Erikka ran past her mother. In the living room, Inga and Annie and Bengt were all sitting on the couch in their pajamas, with their six skinny ankles sticking out like stops on a pipe organ. Their faces showed fear and the traces of tears, and also poorly disguised enthusiasm at the excitement of an argument and staying up late.

Mrs. Knorr went straight to the telephone. Erikka hung up her coat and stood in the doorway. Inga went by to get a glass of water.

"You're really in for it. She was *crying*," whispered Inga daringly as she passed. Erikka resisted an impulse to give her a fierce kick.

"Was she kidnapped?" called Annie at the top of her lungs.

"I wasn't. Go to bed, Annie," said Erikka.

"You're not my mother and you're not in charge of me. You're in trouble 'cause you're kidnapped."

"I am not kidnapped."

Inga came back. "What happened? Where did you go? You can play with my jigsaw puzzle if you're sent to your room."

"I went to see my friend Simon, and we had some business to do," said Erikka.

"BUSINESS?" Mrs. Knorr's voice rose even higher. She had finished calling Mr. Knorr's boss to tell him Erikka was back. "Just what sort of business are you engaged in? And who is this Simon character?" She stood, a judge, a prosecutor, a gallows hand, arms folded, chin firm, eyes piercing. Erikka had never seen her so angry.

"Simon Cameron is a friend of mine who goes to the Dearborn School."

"How old is he?" Mrs. Knorr's face grew white, and suddenly she scooped up Bengt and Annie, one under each arm, and headed down the hall. "Inga, bedtime. *Now.*"

Inga knew there was no arguing at a time like this. She reached out and touched Erikka on the shoulder. "Good luck. I'll stay awake so you can tell me everything." She turned and fled to Erikka's bedroom, where Mrs. Knorr was tucking Annie in.

Erikka was glad she hadn't kicked Inga. She started to cry.

Mrs. Knorr came back down the hall. Erikka watched her coming. She sloped a little to the left, and her face looked hard and ridged, like the trunk of a tree. She straightened up, though, and when she walked into the room there was no mistaking her authority.

"Sit," she said.

Erikka sat.

Mrs. Knorr untied her apron and handed it over. "Wipe your eyes and stop your sniffing. Now, tell me about this Simon."

"He's nothing new, I've known him for months, Mommy," said Erikka. She started winding her fingers in the strings of the apron.

"And you were with him this whole time?"

Erikka decided the truth was best at a time like this. "No. I went to see him after school, and we made our plans, and then I went down to the museum shop at the Art Institute, and then I went back to Simon's and we went to see some people who live on Lake Shore Drive, and then I came home."

"Did Simon hurt you? Or touch you?"

"Of course not." Erikka was mystified. "He's about my best friend, Mommy."

"How old is he?"

"I don't know—same as me, probably. Twelve."

Mrs. Knorr sat down on the couch. Her color started to come back. I've made it through the worst part, thought Erikka.

"Why haven't I met him?"

"Because he goes to that strict school—he lives there. It's a boarding school. He doesn't get to go out much."

"And what were you doing down at the museum shop?"

"I wanted to buy a present for Aunt Kristina."

"What for?"

Erikka stared. "Because I like her. Because I want to."

Mrs. Knorr looked away. "Well, she certainly deserves it tonight. She gave up an important dinner engagement because you never showed up after school, and she's out right now searching for you. I hope she comes in soon. Erikka, you really ought to be ashamed of yourself."

The crying had stopped. "But, Mommy, it was important."

"What was so important that you don't bother to come home till nine o'clock at night, I want to know?"

Erikka took a deep breath, and then plunged into the tale of the Pruitts and Mr. Tolyukov. Mrs. Knorr sat back and listened. When Erikka had finished, her mother said, "I think you spend a great deal of time with your nose in other people's business. Perhaps if I make Tolyukov's bookstore off limits to you, you'll learn your lesson."

"Oh, Mommy, don't!" cried Erikka. "That's the only place I like to go."

"I'll think about it. Do you know that I missed my class tonight because you didn't come home from school? First I take Monday off to be here when Aunt Kristina comes, and then today I have to stay home and wait for you! Do you know how worried you had me?"

"I can take care of myself."

"Oh, you can? Can you put food on the table? Can you

manage the bills and the housework as well as you manage other people's affairs?"

"Well," said Erikka, impatient suddenly with all this fuss, "I used to make suppers for Inga and Annie after my first mother died, before you married Daddy."

Mrs. Knorr jumped off the couch. "To bed!" she cried. "I'll smack you for your insolence in a minute!"

They both heard the downstairs door open. It was Aunt Kristina, who, as she trudged upstairs, called, "Any news?"

"She's back," said Mrs. Knorr.

"Oh, good. Where were you, love?"

"Don't you 'love' her, Kristina, she's in disgrace. Now, Erikka, go to bed."

Erikka looked at Kristina for a moment before turning to leave. In her pine-green coat and snowy scarf, Kristina looked like a woman capable of great mystery and accomplishment. Erikka was flattered at the thought of lovely Kristina peering down dark alleys for her.

"I'm sorry you missed your dinner engagement on my account," said Erikka. Aunt Kristina smiled forgivingly. Erikka left the room.

"She's totally thoughtless," said Mrs. Knorr to Aunt Kristina. Erikka lingered in the dark shadows of the hall to hear Kristina's rebuttal, but her aunt didn't say a word one way or the other.

Despite her best intentions, Inga had not managed to stay awake. When Erikka finished washing up, she stole quietly into her bedroom. Tonight I would like to be by myself, she thought, irritated by the intrusion of the cots and the clothes and Toby the rocking horse in what had been her nice, neat room. I wish I were all alone, so I could sit and be quiet and think; I wish I could feel just my own heart beating in this room, I wish I could sing out loud or be silent, just as I liked, instead of having to adjust myself to these others.

Annie's blanket had fallen off. Erikka picked it up and covered her with it. Then she gingerly climbed over the two cots to her own bed, which was shoved up against the wall.

For a while she just sat there, with her back against the wall and her knees drawn up under her chin. With her tongue she touched the faded red roses on the sleeves of the flannel nightgown, thinking: Where is my holy determination? The failure with the Pruitts and the fight with her mother had left her tired; she only wished that something right would happen, that maybe some of what she had tried to do would eventually work out for somebody's good.

After a time, the misunderstanding and misery having accumulated into a heaviness in her heart, she got up and found the matches in the bottom dresser drawer and lit the candle in the old golden candlestick. She put it in front of the painting and held on to it tightly.

I want to go to the night mountain, she thought.

The moon in the painting, the quarter moon, shone

with the color of old paper, exactly the same color as the flame flickering in her hands. The thick, anxious branches brushed against each other, and the wind caught at her hair, twining it around her neck. With one hand she protected the flame, and with the other she held the heavy candlestick, and then she was pressing into the resisting pine boughs, moving, pouring herself into the woods.

And on the mountainside stood Theresa, in her rough skirt and hiking boots, with a staff in one hand. "Daughter!" she said.

Erikka walked slowly toward her, careful not to let the wind at the flame.

"I know you are coming tonight!" said Theresa gladly. "You are a sight for sore eyes, surely."

"Hello," said Erikka. Oh, no, she thought.

"You come right out of nothing, you appear like a ghost with that strange candle," said Theresa. "Why do you hold it so close?"

"It's the flame of it that keeps me here," said Erikka, and she was speaking about something that she had not consciously been considering but must have been figuring out in her deep, silent mind. The words surprised even herself. "I must guard the flame. When it goes out, I am brought back. But if it goes out when I am not holding it —or when I am somewhere other than right by this tree—I don't know what would happen. It's best not to take chances."

"Tonight is chilly," said Theresa. Her head bobbed from her neck, like a puppy's head. She had put on a cluster of jewels, necklaces and brooches, which were old and tarnished and glittery, and which looked lovely in themselves but silly against the blue flannel shirt and dark shawl Theresa wore.

"You notice my ornaments," said Theresa proudly. "Old family things. I put them on just for you." She smiled. "But tonight is chilly. You come to my little home, we have some tea; we talk about this, about that."

I want to be alone here, said Erikka forcefully to herself, one word at a time. I want to come here and look around by myself and have it be my magic place all alone. I don't want to have tea with a woman older than Noah who wears clunky fake jewelry and hiking boots. I don't want to come all the way here for that.

"Is it far?" said Erikka. "Because you know I can't take any chance on getting stuck here."

"It is not far at all: ten, fifteen minutes through the woods. And that is at my snail's pace. No, do not fear anything, Erikka my daughter, I think about you a great deal since the first time I see you in the woods. I think perhaps I am crazy, like they say about me, but seeing you again in such vividness proves to me that I am not. Or if I am, it is a craziness as real as real life, and so I will not worry about it. But I also am thinking that you do not come this magic way to visit me if you are not meant to talk to me, and if we are not meant to be friends. So come, and for an hour have some tea. Then I will bring you back and you go home."

"All right," said Erikka, feeling obligated.

They made their way through the woods, over which the violent forces of winter and spring seemed to be battling. The trees sported a few buds, and there were shoots and stalks of things thrusting up through the snow; but the wind was still icy, and Erikka could see her breath in the air, by the light of the quarter moon. She was shivering in her nightgown until Theresa took off her dark brown shawl and folded it over her shoulders. They kept on, through groves and brambles and stands of pines, over rocks and boulders and narrow rushing streams; all the time Erikka shielded the flame of the candle with her left hand.

"Now it's just through here," said Theresa, lifting a dead branch so that Erikka could slip underneath it.

Erikka stopped short.

"Now I know this is a dream!" she said fervently.

In the clearing sat a small house with a low roof and small windows. The moon's white light struck the chimney and the smoke rising from it; the moon's light touched the house and the clearing, and left the surrounding forest in shadow. It was like a cottage in a fairy tale, isolated in a magic wood, blessed and enchanted.

Erikka ran forward in delight, Theresa's shawl slipping off her shoulders, the candle tilting dangerously.

"Erikka, mind the flame!"

The girl stopped and uprighted the candlestick. The flame had nearly gone out. She cupped her hand around it till it burned steadily again.

Theresa caught up with her, breathing heavily.

"You pay attention to the flame. We are in a fix if you get stuck here and must call your parents by the long-distance telephone to come and get you."

"I'm sorry."

"Let's go in. You shiver." Theresa entered and Erikka followed.

Inside, Theresa took the candle from Erikka and set it in the center of a table. Then she lit other candles and kerosene lamps around the room; with each burst of flame, the room opened itself up to Erikka.

She turned around and around, clutching the hem of her flannel nightgown in excitement. With the sound of waves a fire hissed in a great stone fireplace; Theresa hung a black kettle on a hook over the flames and added a couple of logs to the blaze. On the wall were ropes of onions and bunches of dried herbs, all around the room, behind which spidery shadows contorted. In a corner was a mattress on a low bedstead, with pillows and a patch-work comforter. There were no cabinets, no closets; things stood on shelves and hung from hooks and nails and rafters. There was a small table and two chairs, up close to the fire, and on the table sat a couple of teacups and a loaf of bread. Theresa didn't say a word while Erikka twisted and stared. She merely took a knife from a hook and cut up the bread, humming some mournful minor melody that Erikka found immensely cheerful.

There was a wooden box under a window, with a lock,

and a key in the lock. Erikka was drawn to that; her fingers itched to turn the key and hear the padlock snap open.

But all she heard instead was the hissing of the fire and the ticking of a clock hidden somewhere in the dark corners.

"Tea," said Theresa, after a while.

Erikka sat in a chair by the fire and put her feet on the warm hearthstone. Chilly and crusted with mud and gravel, her feet steamed a little in the heat.

"Oh, to live alone," Erikka breathed. "With your best books on a shelf, and your onions hanging like treasures from the ceiling. You must be wonderfully happy."

"I am happy to have you come to visit," said Theresa solemnly. She poured into two cups a little dark tea from a china pot on the table. Then she filled the cups with boiling water from the kettle on the hook, and spooned in two teaspoons of strawberry jam. "I am too long alone."

"I don't believe that is possible," said Erikka, suddenly feeling a little friendly. "I have two sisters and a brother, and sometimes I wish I were all grown up, so I could live by myself, quiet and organized, surrounded by beautiful things—paintings, and mountains, and music, and strings of onions."

"Your sisters and your brother are your real treasures," said Theresa.

"The Three Terrors is what I call them." Erikka folded her hands about the teacup and leaned over it, feeling its sweet steam moisten her chin and neck. "I don't hate them. Usually I like them. But I like to be alone."

"Everyone does, at times." Theresa spread some jam on the bread and offered it to Erikka. "I am here for fifteen years, alone almost all the time, and I am not more grateful but for this bit of company now; I am glad you come."

"Fifteen years!" echoed Erikka. "That's a bit longer than I can even imagine about yet."

Theresa tucked a straggling gray hair into place and leaned over. "Your tea; drink up, daughter, it warms."

Erikka lifted the cup to her lips.

She might yet be a witch, and this might be poisoned, Erikka thought fleetingly.

But the look on Theresa's face was one of concern, not malice, so she drank some tea. It was sweet and grainy; the jam had melted into the orangy brew. It was better than regular tea, and Erikka told her so.

"Good," said Theresa.

Erikka kept her hands around the cup to warm them. This room was a charm. If only she could be in it alone, to read, to stir the fire with the poker, to watch the rain, when it rained, from this chair. To sleep on that humble bed. To wake up all alone. Even now was almost perfect— except for Theresa and her humming, which sounded like purring. The pendant draped around the old woman's neck had dipped into the teacup she was holding close. She was absorbed in something.

"That candlestick is fascinating," said Theresa. She looked at it oddly, with a distant concentration. "Where do you get it?"

"A friend," said Erikka.

"Is good friend," said Theresa. "Ah, me, I am getting old, daughter. Time seems to fold back on itself sometimes, and I turn my head and see something I do not think of in many years. When you grow old, Erikka, you live many lives at once. It is rich, but it is perplexing."

You are perplexing, thought Erikka.

"You are a delight," said Theresa suddenly, fishing her pendant from her cup and dangling it so the drops of tea splattered the table. "It is good to have company."

"I'd like to be alone here, I think," said Erikka.

"Ah, no, you would become tired with loneliness."

"No, I wouldn't."

"Yes, you do. I tell you. I know." Theresa smiled.

Erikka felt obstinate. "I would not. I get sick of my brother and sisters sometimes. There's too much noise. I can't even think."

"You think too much, you go crazy."

"You don't think enough and you go crazy, too," said Erikka. "If I were you, I wouldn't even have invited me here tonight. I'd have sat here all alone and done exactly whatever I wanted."

"You are saucy and young. You don't know."

"I do, too. People are just trouble, most of them. Always on your back."

"I would give the treasure of the world to have someone on my back," cried Theresa. "You have the wealth of ages and you don't know it."

"Some wealth. Some treasure." Erikka's tea suddenly

tasted bitter and she didn't want any more. She stood up. "It would be real wealth to me to be able to come here and walk around by myself, and look at things alone, and be alone for a while."

Theresa's face went white.

"I'm going," said Erikka. She grabbed the candle and headed for the door. "Thanks for the tea. See you around."

Theresa's hands went to her necklace. "Daughter, here, don't be angry. Take this—a present. My necklace."

But the anger that had boiled all day, in school, at the Pruitts', at home, was too great in Erikka. She just said, "No, thank you," primly, and left the cottage.

"Well!" shouted Theresa after her. "Well! Well!"

Erikka had a misery like a bad cold in her head. She hadn't meant to be mean to Theresa. After all, the tea was nice, and the invitation was kind, and even if Theresa was old enough to be her great-grandmother, she was still a pleasant woman.

The path was clearly marked, and Erikka balanced the candle high, so as to shed more light. Well, she wouldn't worry about it now. And anyway, she'd been telling the truth. She'd rather come to this astonishing night world to be alone. There were enough problems with people at home; she didn't need any here, too.

At the clearing, she turned to see if Theresa had followed her. Only the sound of the wind high in the trees. No sound of old woman.

So Erikka turned and walked into the dense pine trees. The needles scraped at her through her nightgown, but she thrust herself along, the candlestick held high. Just at the darkest point, the wind whistled—echoes of Theresa's mournful melody, Erikka thought—and the flame was extinguished and the dark fell behind her and she was standing in her own bedroom.

The candle was much shorter; it was half gone now.

Inga was sprawled on her cot, sleeping noisily.

Annie appeared at the door. Her eyes were large.

"Where were you?" she demanded. "Were you kidnapped?"

Erikka shivered, and instinctively pulled the shawl around her—Theresa's shawl.

"Get in bed, or I'll tell Mommy," she said in a sharp voice. Annie ran and jumped on her cot. Erikka sat down on the side of the cot and covered her little sister up. "I went for a walk in the deep deep woods," she sang in a whisper, stroking Annie's hair, and pulling her thumb out of her mouth. "In the deep deep woods, in the deep dark woods, in the dark, in the deep, in the sleepy woods."

She sang in a minor melody, a mournful tune. Soon Annie slept, and Erikka, exhausted, hid Theresa's shawl in her bottom drawer and crawled into bed.

Chapter Seven

THE DAUGHTER
OF THE MOON

School the next day was terrible.

Surprise tests in science and history—Erikka felt insulted by the teachers for doing such a cheap and obvious thing. She couldn't summon any interest in the tests; she did them quickly and casually, as if she were filling out a questionnaire. During English they had grammar instead of literature or writing, and it was so boring that Erikka felt inclined to rip out every page of her grammar book and shower the teacher with appropriate confetti. Then, in math, Sister Xaviera was called out of the room and they were given busy work to do. This is prison, Erikka thought, drawing pictures of candlesticks on the front of her math text. I am so bored I think I might faint from it.

When Sister Xaviera returned and found no work from Erikka Knorr, detention was assigned.

At lunch Doreen told Erikka about a piano concert she had been taken to the night before. The way things were going, Erikka knew that she didn't have to bother asking Doreen if it had been good, or exciting, or tragic, or boring. Doreen hadn't listened. She had spent the evening in a competition with the girl at the ticket window to see who could blow the biggest bubble-gum bubbles.

Inga sought out Erikka on the playground and repeated the news that their second mother had been crying the night before when Erikka hadn't arrived home from school. Erikka thanked Inga for this reminder with a kick. Inga laughed and ran off.

The afternoon did not improve. Instead of Music, they had Lecture, which was what the music teacher did when she couldn't make the class sing in tune. Erikka began to get impatient.

"I saw your name on the detention list," Inga whispered to Erikka as they passed each other in the hall. "Do you want me to tell Mommy you have to stay after?"

"Might as well," said Erikka wearily.

Detention was not so bad, though. It lasted forty-five minutes after the other students had been released. The history teacher sat with a cup of coffee and talked under his breath to the English teacher, who was laughing and trying not to show it in front of the detention students. Erikka ignored them and finished up her math assignment quickly.

When it was time to go, she raced out the door.

For the first time all day, she was awake. She ran for two blocks to get away from St. Mary's, and when she finally stopped for breath, leaning up against the window of a dry cleaner's, things swam into a clearer focus than usual.

"Hey—don't lean on the glass. Move on," shouted someone from inside the dry cleaner's.

It's no good running, Erikka thought, her eyes filling with tears. I can't get away from this grayness, this ugliness. It's not like a wall, it's not like a monster; it's nameless, faceless, and total as a fog. It lives in Chicago like a disease that never goes away.

A bus went by; a tangible tail of gritty exhaust trailed after it. Erikka sat on a step.

It's not just the air. It's not just the filth. It's in people, and in their lives. It shows on their faces like the Kiss of Death. Erikka didn't remember where she had heard about the Kiss of Death, but it was appropriate as a title for what she hated about Chicago.

On their faces. In their lives. In the heavy, tired way people are walking on this street; in the heavy way buildings stand and stare.

Was she like that, too? Did some of that rank plague touch her? Could it be that she was cross, and impatient, and feeling like stones were inside her sometimes, because of the infectious chilliness around her?

I know I have good in me, she said fervently to herself. I know there's something worthwhile here. It's in me, stuck, and if it doesn't come out I'll get old and uninterested in everything, and work at a job and just trudge instead of dance, and just croak instead of sing, and wear gray aprons instead of skirts. What if that happens? If I only think about potatoes boiling and the rent, instead of trees and wind and being alive? I can almost feel it happening already—I'm turning dark and old and stiff, dull and dead as this concrete step I'm sitting on.

I could die and not even know it.

Suddenly, as fast as they had come, the tears left her. Erikka stood up. An old lady was walking by, carrying a heavy grocery bag.

"Get along, girl, you don't belong here," said the old lady, not even looking at her as she walked up the steps that Erikka had been sitting on.

Erikka didn't answer. She just started walking. With dignity and purpose, she walked evenly away.

I have just crossed a bridge in my life, and I will never go back, she said to herself, striding steadily down Merriam Street. I will not stay here. I will not live here. I don't know where I will go and I certainly can't go when I'm only twelve years old, but I know this: I am going to leave here as soon as I am old enough. I am going to try to be as fully alive as I can.

Erikka did not see Florry waving hello from behind the counter in the Merriam Deli under her home. She just walked steadily on, up the stairs to their apartment.

"Ah, Erikka," said Mrs. Knorr sadly, "why did you have to stay after today?"

"I didn't finish a math assignment," said Erikka, taking off her coat. "But I got it done after school."

"I know that you try hard, Erikka," said her mother.

"But I wanted you to come home right away after school today. Now I've been waiting for you so you could mind Bengt and Annie while I run out and get a few things for supper."

"Why couldn't Inga mind them?" asked Erikka.

"She's gone to the post office for me."

"All right." Erikka sat down at the kitchen table and looked straight ahead.

"They're playing down in your bedroom. Erikka, do you feel well?" Mrs. Knorr paused with her coat halfway on and crossed the kitchen. Her hand went to Erikka's forehead.

Erikka didn't say anything.

"You seem a little warm to me. I hope you're not coming down with anything, not while Aunt Kristina's here. I'll take your temperature as soon as I get back. Now where's that list?" She searched her pockets.

"Is this it—hamburger, rice, toilet paper, toothpaste—" read Erikka from a scrap of paper she'd found on the table.

"That's it. Now go mind the little ones. I'll be back in a flash." Mrs. Knorr hurried down the stairs. Erikka sat still and heard the bottom door close.

Annie and Bengt were playing witch and monster on Erikka's bed: Annie was both the witch and monster, and Bengt was the audience. Erikka chased them both off her bed, and then she stretched out on it. Annie and Bengt climbed on Inga's cot.

"I am witch and I eat people with big knees!" screamed Annie. Bengt crowed with delight, his hands on his knees.

"Monster is good friend of witch. I am monster and I push babies off bed!" Annie enacted the scene convincingly. Bengt screamed his lines of pain and rage from the floor.

"Don't push Bengt off the bed!" yelled Erikka in exasperation.

"He likes it," said Annie.

"He doesn't," said Erikka. "Come here, Bengt." She pulled the baby up onto her lap. He crawled off immediately.

"Let's play Indians. I'll be an Indian on my horse," decided Annie. She scrambled onto Toby and galloped at top speed in the doorway. "You be the witch."

"I won't be the witch."

"You be the witch," commanded Annie, "and Bengt can be a pancake."

"No," said Erikka. "Get off Toby and come here. I'll tell you a story. I'll tell you about Sleeping Beauty."

"No. I'll tell *you* a story." Annie ran over and catapulted herself onto the bed.

"Okay. Start."

"Once upon a time," said Annie.

"Go on."

"You tell it."

"No. You said you were going to and you do it."

"I don't want to." Annie's lower lip started to tremble.

"Oh, don't cry! I'll do it. Once upon a time, in a deep dark forest, there was a castle."

"*I'll* tell it!" screamed Annie. "Once upon a time was a deep castle with dark in it."

"Yes?"

"Do you want to eat the pancake?" Annie asked, looking hopefully at Bengt.

"Oh, you little stinker! I'm going to eat you!" threatened Erikka, tickling her.

"Can we play with your light?" asked Annie, with a pillow on her head.

"My what?"

"Light. LIGHT," said Annie clearly.

"What light?" asked Erikka casually.

"Your LIGHT!" said Annie, pointing at the Russian candlestick.

"Let's have a cookie! Do you want a cookie, Annie?"

"Yes." Annie bounced up and down on Erikka's bed.

"Well, come on. Bengt, do you want a cookie? Bengt want cookie?" Erikka gathered Bengt up in her arms; he laughed and pulled her hair.

"Come on," ordered Annie. "I'll go first." She flung herself down the hall.

Erikka looked around. Perhaps she ought to hide Tolyukov's candlestick some place.

"How can a pancake eat a cookie?" called Annie from the kitchen.

She *would* hide it, after supper tonight.

"Cookie!" Annie reminded her, at the top of her lungs. Erikka went and dug up some cookies for her and Bengt.

When Aunt Kristina let herself into the apartment a while later, she found the four children finishing the last of the cookies. Annie had spilt some milk, and so the sheet of stamps that Inga had bought at the post office were all stuck to the tabletop.

"Where's your mother?" asked Aunt Kristina.

"Shopping for dinner."

"Oh, good—look, I brought her a surprise." Aunt Kristina put down a box on the table and opened it up. "Look out, Bengt, let me see," complained Inga.

It was a box of short-stemmed yellow roses.

"Oh, pretty!" screamed Annie, reaching for the blossom of the nearest one and mangling it beyond recognition. Aunt Kristina swept the rest of them out of the box and up to her face. Erikka stared in overwhelming admiration. Kristina was as beautiful a woman as ever she had seen, yellow roses or none.

And Mommy won't give them a second glance, she thought ruefully. They'll be wasted on her.

"A vase—a smallish vase. Erikka, where does your mother keep her vases?"

"She doesn't have any," admitted Erikka, embarrassed. "My good blue one that used to be my first mother's isn't here right now. And our second mother doesn't own any. She uses an empty peanut-butter jar when Annie and Bengt bring her dandelions and grass."

"She does, too," protested Inga. "The white barber's bottle that she told us once was her own mother's. The one in the front room."

"You're right. It'll be perfect, Inga," said Kristina warmly. Erikka was angry at herself for forgetting about the barber's bottle.

"See if you can pry loose those stamps, Erikka," suggested Kristina. "I'll get the vase. We'll have a pretty bouquet on the table for your mother when she gets home from shopping."

"Let's play witch!" Annie said to Bengt, and they raced away to Erikka's bedroom.

Inga fingered the mutilated rose. "I think I'll stick this in my prayer book and pretend it was given to me by Tom Higgins."

"You'll need more than prayers to get a rose from Tom Higgins," said Erikka, scraping at the stuck stamps with a knife.

"Roses are red, violets are blue," said Inga. "You're just mad because you don't have a boyfriend. You're an old maid."

Erikka threw the knife in the sink and turned to her younger sister. "It's better than pretending," she said calmly. "I would take that rose and throw it out. I'd rather wait for a perfect, uncrushed rose that Annie hadn't destroyed than make do with a mess and pretend it was all right."

"*De gustibus non est disputandum,*" said Inga smartly.

Kristina had just come in the room with Mrs. Knorr's precious white vase. She started to laugh. "What are you talking about?"

"*De gustibus non est disputandum,*" repeated Erikka. "Mommy always says that when Annie says that the broccoli tastes awful. It means that there can't be any arguing about whether or not something tastes good or bad. What tastes good to me might taste bad to Annie."

"She *knows* what it means," said Inga.

"Actually, I didn't," admitted Kristina. "But it makes sense."

"Hmmph," said Inga. "A rose is a rose, dead or alive."

"Rattle on about roses, that's right," said Erikka. "Meanwhile, notice these stamps, twenty of them, ruined and ripped by your carelessness, Inga."

"Annie spilt the milk, not me."

"You left them on the table, not her."

"How does that look?" asked Aunt Kristina.

She set the bottle on the table, and the seven yellow roses were bright against the greens like canaries in a jungle.

"Oh, Aunt Kristina, they are exquisite," said Erikka. "I wish we had some place better to put them than on this old kitchen table. Why don't we put them on the bookcase?"

"No one would look at them there," said Kristina. "No —let's leave them here where everyone can enjoy them."

Inga went downstairs to pay Florry back a quarter she

owed. Kristina fiddled with the roses for a few minutes, rearranging them with great concentration.

"How do you know when it's right?" asked Erikka.

"Well—when it looks right. When it looks balanced. It's hard to explain. I look at it. See, if this one in the back is four inches higher than all the others, it looks as if it's going to tip over. So I push it down, but then the back looks too crowded. So I rearrange them like this. There's no one way—I just keep at it till it seems right. There—how's that?"

"Looks fine to me."

"Me too." Kristina smiled at Erikka. "I've got to get ready for a dinner engagement tonight."

Erikka followed her aunt down the hall and into Inga's and Annie's bedroom. Kristina closed the door and Erikka flopped down on Annie's bed.

"Do you like this city?" asked Erikka.

Aunt Kristina paused at the closet door and turned around.

"I like to visit you," she said.

"No, I know that. I mean, do you like Chicago?"

Aunt Kristina rummaged through the closet where her clothes were hung. "Chicago is exciting in some respects. There are a lot of people, a lot of ideas, a lot of things to do."

She pulled out a skirt and held it to her waist. It was a soft blue wool thing with folds like the waves of an ocean. *"C'est jolie, n'est-ce pas?"*

Erikka smiled.

"Tell me what you think of Chicago," said Aunt Kristina, beginning to undress.

"I hate it. It seems ugly and dead. It might have been beautiful once, but it is terrible now. At night, you can't even see the stars—just an orange glow from all the street lights. There's always a gray sky—what good is it getting up in the morning when the sun never really rises? I hate it, Aunt Kristina. I want to go some place where the people look at each other instead of ignoring each other."

"Darling!" Aunt Kristina drew off her panty hose and draped them over the edge of Inga's bed. "You have never lived anyplace else, have you?"

"No," said Erikka. "Once before my first mother died, we went on a camping trip up to Wisconsin. But other than that, I've always lived in this house."

"How do you know anyplace else would be better?"

"It has to be. I just know it." Erikka sat up and traced the design of Annie's bedspread. "Like the way you know when the roses aren't arranged right, and when they are— I know that this isn't right, the way people live here."

"Where do you want to live?"

"In your painting!" Erikka was reckless. "With a bright moon and stars that really shine instead of just fizzling, and with trees that grow where they will instead of where they're planted."

"That's just a painting," said Kristina softly.

"It isn't!" insisted Erikka. "You painted it from a photograph of a real place."

"Well, so I did. But you can't fall in love with a painting, Erikka."

"It's what the painting represents that I love," said Erikka, thinking for just a moment about telling her aunt of the magic, and then deciding against that idea.

"Oh, wise woman!" said Kristina, not unkindly, pulling her sweater off over her head. "I do know what you mean. But it's not all cut-and-dried. There are hard things about living in the country as well as in the city. People there can be cold and uncaring and stupid. And people in the city can be warm and interesting and alive. It's not where you live, it's who you are."

"No," said Erikka. "Who you are is part of it. But where you live must affect you, too; I know that."

"You must know some wonderful people here," said Kristina. "Come on—name them for me."

"Mr. Tolyukov, the bookseller. Francisco, the violinist who lives in an apartment next door. Simon Cameron."

"And . . . what about your mother and father? And Inga and Annie and Bengt?"

"My mother and father are nice people. But they aren't wonderful."

Aunt Kristina had completely undressed. Thinking about her first mother, Erikka looked at her aunt's lovely skin and pleasant woman's form; her long blond hair was swept up and pinned loosely on top of her head, and its straying hairs seemed like light, holy light, on her.

"You are wonderful, Aunt Kristina. I'm glad you're here now. I'm glad you gave me that painting."

Kristina smiled, and her eyes glistened.

"Why did you call me the daughter of the moon? Are you the daughter of the moon?" whispered Erikka.

Kristina turned and put her palms to her forehead. The line of her backbone suddenly reminded Erikka of the stem of a yellow rose; and her head bent forward like a blossom. Will I be as beautiful, Erikka wondered.

"The daughter of the moon," said Kristina, after a minute. "The image comes from an old rhyme." She turned around and sat down close to Erikka, reaching for and touching her hands.

"Listen," she said.

> *"Luna, every woman's friend,*
> *To me thy goodness condescend.*
> *Let this night in visions see*
> *Emblems of my destiny."*

She sat still, close and warm. Erikka breathed reverently the full good smell of her naked body—like the aroma of a rose, she thought dazedly.

"Do you understand that rhyme?" asked Aunt Kristina.

"No," Erikka said.

"Well. Luna means the moon, in Latin. The poem is being said by a woman to the moon. I'll paraphrase it: Moon, my friend, give me your goodness. Tonight, in my dreams, let me see pictures of my future life."

"Oh," said Erikka.

"I found that rhyme when I was researching a book of nursery rhymes I wanted to illustrate." Kristina looked off to one side. "It was my favorite. And the daughter of the moon just refers, in my own thinking, to a woman who is moved by the beauty of things, by the beauty of the moon.

"So I guess that you are a daughter," Kristina continued.

Erikka felt she had just received a blessing. She lowered her head and blushed.

"Lovely one," said Aunt Kristina. She leaned over and kissed Erikka's forehead. Then she got up and started rummaging through her suitcase.

"Erikka?" Mrs. Knorr was knocking on the bedroom door.

"Come in," said Kristina.

Mrs. Knorr entered, her coat still on.

"Goodness, Kristina, what are you doing?" she said in a high voice.

"Oh—I'm getting dressed to go out. Erikka and I were just having a nice talk."

"Well, please, Kristina, a little modesty!" Mrs. Knorr sounded quite upset. Erikka looked up at her. Puzzlement and dismay showed on her bony face. "Erikka, please don't bother your aunt. I thought I asked you to mind Bengt and Annie. Now, no more talking to your aunt, not while she's dressing."

Kristina threw on a robe quickly. "I'm sorry, Sharon, I didn't realize it would upset you."

"I'm not upset. But this apartment is large enough to afford you a little privacy. Come, Erikka, at once."

Erikka stood. Her mother was looking at Aunt Kristina with some unfathomable feelings flashing. Her aunt stood nobly with her head high and her arms crossed in front of her. A battle? Enemies or friends? Maybe Mommy doesn't like Aunt Kristina, Erikka thought suddenly.

"Do what your mother says," suggested Kristina.

Erikka left the room reluctantly. She had felt like a special friend to Aunt Kristina for a few minutes, and was sorry to let go of that warmth. Kristina was busy smoothing out her skirt. Mrs. Knorr stood awkwardly, like a guardian uncomfortable with her task, uncomfortable in her own home. When Erikka left, Mrs. Knorr pulled the bedroom door closed behind her.

"Now, Erikka, I think you ought to have a little soup and go to bed early. You don't act as if you're in the pink of health," said Mrs. Knorr.

"I am perfectly fine." Erikka's tone was chilly.

"Where is Inga? And why aren't you minding Bengt and Annie as I asked you to?"

"Because everyone else was home, except for you."

Annie and Bengt came charging out of Erikka's bedroom and down the hall, chanting and slamming. They rushed past Mrs. Knorr and Erikka at full speed into the kitchen.

"Oh, stop!" cried Erikka, and leaped forward.

The crash resounded throughout the apartment. Inga,

letting herself in, dashed upstairs with the front door flapping wide open to Merriam Street. And Aunt Kristina arrived last, in her long blue dressing gown.

Bengt was laughing in delight, but Annie was old enough to know trouble when it came. The seven yellow roses lay in a heap of greens and shards of glass against the baseboard. The precious barber's bottle was broken in angry pointed pieces.

"Bengt did it, not me," said Annie in a little voice.

Mrs. Knorr just stared. "Roses in the kitchen? In my good bottle? Who did that?"

Aunt Kristina hurried to her. "Sharon, it was my fault. I'm so sorry. Please forgive me. I brought you roses tonight—"

"Roses!" said Mrs. Knorr.

"Look, the roses aren't broken," said Annie, stooping to check.

"Roses!" yelled Bengt happily.

"Roses on the kitchen table! Kristina, are you out of your mind?" Mrs. Knorr was incredulous. "Four children in the house and you bring home roses? And put them in my barber's bottle? Kristina, that belonged to my mother for fifty years! I've only had it since she died last November! It was one of her favorite things. And it's broken."

Nobody said anything.

I knew she wouldn't appreciate them, thought Erikka.

"What's for supper?" Annie asked, tactfully changing the subject.

"And you," said Mrs. Knorr, suddenly gripping Erikka's shoulder with great strength. "If you had been minding those little ones, the way you were supposed to, this wouldn't have happened. I hope you're pleased with yourself."

"Really, Sharon, it was my stupidity," said Aunt Kristina. "I ought to have thought—"

"You kids go to your rooms," said Mrs. Knorr in an odd high voice. They all fled to Erikka's room, except Inga, who went downstairs to close the street door (and to slip into the deli to tell Florry the bad news). Only Aunt Kristina stayed, helping Mrs. Knorr clean up the mess.

Erikka, Annie, and Bengt all sat on Erikka's bed.

"She's not going to be my mommy any more," said Annie loudly.

"Be quiet, Annie," said Erikka.

"My name isn't Annie. It's Martha Wong."

"Well then, be quiet, Martha Wong."

The three children looked at each other.

"Is she mad? Do you think she's *real* mad?" Annie asked after a while.

"You broke her favorite vase, Annie."

"My name isn't Annie. It's—"

"All right, Martha Wong!"

"I know what. Let's play with your light," suggested Annie, pointing at Tolyukov's candlestick.

"You are not to touch that!" Erikka declared, threateningly.

"You can't tell Martha Wong what to do," taunted Annie. She stuck out her tongue at Erikka, who slapped her. The little girl began to give out great energetic sobs. Loyal Bengt joined in right away.

"Good Lord!" Erikka stuffed a pillow over her head and turned her back on the weeping ones. "The next time I won't come back!"

Chapter Eight

SWEET
SKULDUGGERY

Mrs. Knorr didn't say another word about the broken bottle. She and Aunt Kristina both acted as if it hadn't happened. At dinnertime, the yellow roses were displayed in a peanut-butter jar on the kitchen table. Erikka couldn't help thinking that they were not arranged so carefully as before.

When Erikka awoke the next morning, she felt horrible. Her head pounded and her throat was like sandpaper. But for once, she didn't want to stay home, not with her mother mad at her. So she put on a splendid performance of health and high spirits, helping to feed Bengt, pouring orange juice for everyone.

"She's sick," decided Inga. "Erikka, I can't drink a third glass of orange juice. I'll never make it through first period."

"Want to wear my gray sweater?' asked Erikka brightly.

"Sure. What's the catch?"

"No catch. I'm going to wear my blue one, so my gray one is free if you want it . . ." Erikka dashed down the hall to find it.

"Erikka, I'm not so sure you ought to go to school today. You seem to be coming down with a cold," called Mrs. Knorr.

Just then Annie stomped into the kitchen. "Martha Wong wants her breakfast and she wants it NOW." While Mrs. Knorr was distracted, Inga and Erikka ran outside.

The April wind was warm, and skies were blue for a change. Little points of grass were poking up between the cracks in the sidewalk. Even Inga seemed affected.

"You got some big date after school today?" asked Inga as they crossed Merriam Street.

"No. Why?"

"I just wondered. You didn't leap at the chance to miss a day of school."

"I want to go see my friend Mr. Tolyukov today."

"Hmmm. Is he the only one?"

"Inga, just because you're boy crazy doesn't mean everyone is."

"But . . . oh, forget it," said Inga. "I'm just surprised that you didn't take advantage of a perfectly good chance to miss school."

"I know what you mean," said Erikka. "Today is one day when I actually do feel a little sick, too."

They both laughed.

"Here comes Tom Higgins—do you want me to beat it?" asked Erikka.

"Nah. He's just a jerk. You're my sister," said Inga. They hurried on.

* * *

With a little effort, Erikka managed to get through the day uncriticized by her teachers. When the three o'clock bell rang, she ran out of St. Mary's, past Inga, who was talking to Tom Higgins, past the steps where she had sat and cried yesterday, down to the great hulking Dearborn School for Boys.

Simon was waiting. They had made no arrangements, had set no date, but he seemed to know she would be coming. "About an hour," said Simon. "Things are in an uproar in there. There's flu going around and several of the proctors have it. So I can be safely out for an hour. But at four-thirty today we have inspection, and I can't miss that."

They strode off purposefully toward Tolyukov's bookstore a few blocks away. Erikka told Simon about the yellow-rose-and-barber's-bottle crisis the night before, but he didn't seem very impressed.

"So buy her a new one," he suggested.

"There's always trouble," said Erikka. "I can't seem to avoid it. If it isn't at home, it's over on the mountain—Theresa was a real fuss the night before last."

"Oh," said Simon. "So you're still tripping back and forth from Chicago to some magic mountain?"

"When I feel like it." Erikka loftily ignored the acid disbelief in Simon's voice. "But honestly, with Theresa so opinionated and graspy, I don't have any great desire to go back. It seems so mean: I get this great chance to escape from my family, and then this hobbling old lady has to be there and spoil it all."

Simon kicked a can down the street, his lips pressed together tightly. "Maybe the old lady, if there is one, thinks the same about—"

"Good Lord!" exploded Erikka. But she wasn't answering him; she wasn't paying him a bit of attention. She was staring at Tolyukov's store windows.

The window display was all rearranged; instead of the spread of volumes showing colorful dust jackets or faded bindings, the books were stacked into two pillars, as if they were about to be moved. The Countess Olga Molokiev was stretched out between the piles of books, twitching her whiskers in the warmth.

"What's this?" Simon pointed to a sign on the door.

CLOSING CLEARANCE SALE

Thank you for your patronage

Erikka, wordless, pushed inside.

"More help, I hope," said Tolyukov, pausing to catch his breath, with several books in his arms.

"What are you doing?" said Erikka.

"Having a very uneventful clearance sale," said Tolyukov, "and beginning to pack things up at the same time."

"But why?"

"I'll sell the whole thing, bulk, to some dealer. Keeping aside the best volumes, of course. It's all secondhand stuff; nobody's knocking the doors down to get it even at reduced prices, as you can see for yourselves."

"But— Well, I *know* that. But you're giving up so quickly . . ."

Tolyukov hummed for a minute, thinking. "Did you ever hear the old saying that it's no good flogging a dead horse?" he said softly.

"You're not a dead horse," said Erikka.

"No. But the store is. And at my age, when a change is to be made, it's easier sometimes to make it quickly."

He smiled at both children. "So have you come to help me pack? Since the clearance sale seems to be drawing no customers at all?"

"Sure," said Simon.

"I don't know," said Erikka.

"As you like," said Tolyukov.

"It's not that I don't want to help you," said Erikka quickly. "I just am sorry to see you so . . . decided." And so old, she thought, and looking so terribly lost, even here, with books in odd stacks all around the place. If you look so old now, what will you look like when you've actually given up the store for good? And you never, ever, said you were too old before.

"Your help, I appreciate," Tolyukov said.

"Oh, we've been a great help," said Erikka. "Being the cause of all this in the first place."

"I meant it sincerely, Erikka," the old man said, wiping his hands on a cloth. "Our friend Francisco is over there packing the reference books." Francisco de Medina looked up from his place on the floor and waved. "I need more help, or I'll never be packed in time to leave."

"I don't want you to give in to them," said Erikka, knowing she was becoming a nuisance but unable to contain herself.

Tolyukov sighed. "You don't want to know all my financial woes, Erikka. Loans and debts and overextended credits. I can't comfortably absorb a loss as big as the Pruitts' five-thousand-dollar bill. So the crazy machinery of business stalls and jams and rips its gears.

"After all," he said, turning, "I have my pride. I won't stay in a building if I can't pay the rent. That's wrong."

"But it's the Pruitts who are wrong." Erikka tugged on his sleeve in emphasis. "Go to court. Call a lawyer."

"I can't afford it, the time, the energy, the finances," said Tolyukov. "The Pruitts have the money and expertise to lay down the rules of the game, even if they're illegal rules. They'll pay, eventually, I'm sure. But I could have accumulated several months of bills that would be impossible to pay. And I won't do that. Now, if you'll help a bit?"

"Of course," said Simon. "Just tell us what to do."

"Well," said Tolyukov, "the contemporary novels back there by the radiator need to be inventoried. Those I'll have to send back to the publishers. You want to start on that, Simon?"

Erikka went over to help Francisco.

"I thought that a person studying to be a doctor never had a spare minute," she said.

"I'm glad for an excuse to do something other than study," Francisco answered.

Erikka looked at him, at his black Filipino hair thick and straight as the bristles in a paintbrush, at his goldeny brown skin. "Aren't you sad that Mr. Tolyukov is going?" she said.

"Shh," said the young man in a whisper. "Don't make it harder on old Tolyukov than it is already."

"Erikka, would you make some tea?" asked Tolyukov, from across the room.

Erikka looked at Francisco despairingly. He winked at her. She sighed and jumped up to do what she had been asked.

The back room, the lovely back room, the most perfect back room that a person could live in, was a mess. The few pieces of furniture were pushed up against a side wall, and a great island of cardboard boxes swelled up to the ceiling.

She almost couldn't bear it. Tears started as she ran the water and found teacups in the sink. Tears trickled, but she worked steadily on, sniffling very very quietly. By the time she had arranged the teacups and pot on the old tray with the painting of St. Basil's, she had succeeded in stilling the tears.

"Tea?" she said brightly to the three workers in the front room. My second acting job of the day, she thought. I ought to go on the stage.

"A welcome respite," said Tolyukov.

"I hate tea," said Simon. "I'll just take water."

"Come, Francisco. A little rest." The young man joined them; he and Simon and Erikka sat on the counter, and

Mr. Tolyukov took the stool. For a while nobody spoke. The Countess padded softly over to the counter and leaped up, nestling her head in Erikka's lap.

"Lovely Olga, lovely cat," said Erikka, scratching the cat's ears so that its face squeezed up with pleasure. "Are you looking forward to a move?"

"All she needs, that one, is sun and a few drops of milk," said Tolyukov. "The Countess has only known a life of luxury. She doesn't need me."

"Odd name for a cat," said Francisco. "The Countess?"

"Olga Molokiev," said Erikka and Mr. Tolyukov simultaneously, and they smiled.

"Named for the love of my life that I lost sixty years ago," said Tolyukov. "We were to be married. But we lost contact somehow, with wars and depressions and being a half a world apart. I don't know that she even survived. I don't know that she ever left Russia."

The Countess on the counter sat up regally, displaying classic feline grace and feminine mystery. She turned and looked at Francisco very very slowly, and then jumped gracefully to the floor. She found an empty box and investigated it.

"If my violin was here, I would be playing you something tragic and romantic and Russian," said Francisco.

"Sad music for a sad story," said Simon.

"It's not a story, it's true," objected Erikka.

"Oh, I know," answered Simon.

Erikka finished her tea and looked at the old man, his

arms so thin that his sleeves wouldn't stay rolled up unless he pinned them, his face lined and craggy from the years, his eyes somehow big and fragile in the sunken face.

"Where will you go, Mr. Tolyukov?" Simon asked.

"I am storing my things in a couple of spare rooms that a friend of mine has on the South Side," replied Tolyukov. "For a time I may stay with my friend Martin Van Dyne. A retired Dutch merchant. And after that—well, we'll have to see."

"A true internationalist, this one," said Francisco.

Erikka successfully suppressed an impulse to scream. How could Tolyukov be so calm when his world was coming apart?

Maybe Francisco saw this thought flash on her face. He was silent for a minute, and then he said: "A good idea. Listen. I think my music teacher has extra tickets for tonight's concert at the symphony. Why don't I call him up and see if we can buy them? We can go out and have a soda afterward."

"Oh, yes!" Erikka clapped her hands.

"They'll never allow it," predicted Simon about his guardians at the school.

"I shall insist," said Tolyukov, summoning up such a deep voice, so impressive with its foreign accent, that they all laughed. Francisco made the call right away.

"If we meet here at seven," guessed the old man, "that should be plenty of time to take the el downtown."

* * *

"But you still look sick, Erikka," said Mrs. Knorr. She was about to go out to class, lugging a pile of books and papers, and dressed in her husband's parka.

"Oh, Mommy!" said Erikka in despair. She couldn't even bring herself to say anything else.

"I want to go to symphy," proclaimed Annie. "Bengt does, too."

"Is your homework done?" asked Mrs. Knorr, looking for her keys.

"Yes, and tomorrow's Saturday, anyway, so it's not a school night. And we won't be late, and I'll make them not stop for a soda afterward, and I'll go right to bed when I get home, and I won't be crabby in the morning, I promise, and I'll bring a handkerchief and a dime and I won't talk to strangers or get lost—"

Inga came into the kitchen. "I'll do her dishes for her," she said.

"Has anyone seen my keys? I'm going to be late," said Mrs. Knorr.

"Bengt put your keys in the milk," said Annie solemnly.

"Oh, you little terror!" said Mrs. Knorr. "A half gallon of milk ruined!" She emptied the carton into the sink and quickly rinsed off the keys.

"Why did you waste all that milk? You could have just fished the keys out," said Inga.

Erikka twisted her hair around her left wrist in suspense.

"Now, mind Aunt Kristina, girls," said Mrs. Knorr,

drying the keys. "I'll miss my bus tonight for sure. Florry's not coming up tonight, because your aunt is here. Annie, will you be a good girl for your aunt? Inga, see that she uses the bathroom before she goes to bed. Erikka,"—and by now her mother was running down the stairs—"be sure to thank your friends for their kind invitation. And try not to be too late!" She was gone.

"Martha Wong is going to symphy tonight," Annie said to Bengt. "She's bringing her keys."

Erikka stepped into the Merriam Deli to show Florry how nice she looked. She was wearing her white dress, the one that Mrs. Knorr had bought at the St. Mary's bazaar for a dollar-fifty. It was just plain and white, with white buttons like pearls, simple as snow. Aunt Kristina had arranged her hair in some French fashion, all on top of her head like a hat—Kristina had delayed her own supper to do it, while the Three Terrors made critical remarks over their hot dogs and beans. And then, the final touch— Kristina had loaned her a shawl. A shawl! It was loosely woven from mohair, all soft like the Countess's coat, but egg-white. It fell around her shoulders like a mantle that had been made to order. Inga and Annie and Bengt had been rendered speechless, for a few seconds at least.

Of course, she had to wear her regular ugly green coat; it was much too cold to walk the streets of Chicago at night in just a dress and a soft shawl. But as soon as she got there she would stuff her coat under the seat.

"A picture of perfection!" said Florry, slapping mayonnaise on rye. "Ain't she, folks? Now whaddya think?"

The customers burst into applause. Erikka beamed.

"You look more and more like your first mother every day," said Florry. "Anyone could see it."

Erikka was too surprised at this to answer. It had never occurred to her that she might resemble her first mother. She said goodbye to Florry and left, hurrying down Merriam Street toward the bookstore.

Wouldn't she be proud of me, dressed in white on an April night, thought Erikka. Hurrying to join my friends to go to the symphony? She'd have wanted to come, too.

Not like my mother now. Giving a lecture on cathedral construction. But somehow, Erikka was still so pleased at being allowed to go that she didn't mind what her second mother was doing.

She was anxious for Tolyukov and Francisco and Simon to see her. She ran.

Unfortunately, Simon had been right. The best of Mr. Tolyukov's persuasions weren't enough to convince the people in charge to permit Simon a night at the symphony.

Erikka was crushed. She knew that he liked the excitement of being out at night, of hearing stirring music. I will remember every single detail, Erikka swore to herself, and I will tell him tomorrow.

Francisco and Mr. Tolyukov were both impressed by her appearance, and Erikka was equally taken with them.

Mr. Tolyukov wore a tie. Since he hated ties, Erikka could tell he was trying to make this a special occasion. Francisco wore a navy-blue suit with brass buttons and a white turtleneck.

How elegant we are, said Erikka to herself. An honorable old Russian, a young Filipino violinist-almost-doctor, and a younger American girl, whose hair is piled on her head in a French style. She wondered if everyone on the el would notice. No one did, except a little boy about Annie's age who said to his mother that Erikka looked as if she had a giant mushroom on her head. Erikka didn't care. She smiled sweetly at him when they got up to leave.

"We're in luck," said Francisco as they neared the hall. "This concert has been sold out for months. My music teacher had bought extra tickets for his students, but some canceled out and he hadn't gotten around to returning the extra tickets."

"What will they be playing tonight?" asked Erikka. She couldn't yet tell one composer from another, but she liked to know.

"I'm not sure of the whole thing. The highlight, though, is Beethoven's Piano Concerto in E-flat—the "Emperor" Concerto. The pianist is John Deaconson, who won the Dimitri Mitropoulos music competition last year. He's an American, very good."

Erikka loved the sounds of such words, the look of elegant people hurrying up to the front doors of the hall. She shivered with excitement.

* * *

Francisco sighted some friends of his in the lobby, and he hurried over to say hello. Erikka watched him be greeted with great enthusiasm and warmth, and felt pleased he was so well liked. Then Francisco pointed over to where Tolyukov and Erikka were waiting, by the wall. Tolyukov gave a little wave, but Erikka turned and lifted her head, so Francisco's friends might notice her elegant hair style.

The ushers sat them in the middle of the most expensive section. Everyone sitting around them looked bored, waiting for the program to begin. Erikka had never seen so many double chins assembled in one place at the same time. She didn't see anyone else in the hall who looked anywhere near twelve.

An old lady tapped Tolyukov on the shoulder and leaned forward to say, "Harold and I agree: you have a lovely little girl there."

"Yes, I have," said Tolyukov.

"Shhh!" said several annoyed people, because the orchestra was tuning up.

Erikka glanced over at Francisco. He was sitting as far forward in his seat as possible without crashing to the floor. There was a look of piercing pain on his face; he was concentrating so hard that his eyes were nearly crossed.

Erikka tugged at his sleeve. "What's wrong?" she whispered frantically.

"The second violins—one of them is tuned flat," he answered worriedly.

"How can you tell?"

He didn't answer her; all his attention was directed to the stage. Suddenly he relaxed, slumping back in his seat, exhaling a great relieved sigh.

"He fixed it. Phew."

"How could you tell it was out of tune?"

"I could hear it. You can tell when it's not right."

"I couldn't."

"I could, all too clearly." Francisco shuddered.

Another one of those artist's knowledges—like Aunt Kristina arranging the roses and just knowing when it was right, thought Erikka. "You must be an artist," she said to Francisco.

The old lady seated behind Tolyukov tapped him on the shoulder again. "You'd better keep your lovely little girl quiet or Harold will have to speak to an usher," she said with a polite smile.

"Shh!" said the annoyed people.

The conductor came out from the left. He bowed to the audience, who applauded wildly. Then he turned, picked up his stick, and raised his hands as if signaling a taxi.

When he brought them down, the music began.

It ran through the hall like slow waves from a lazy sea. Eyes closed contentedly, heads nodded, double chins sagged. It was something by a person named Ravel. Erikka glanced at the program. *Pavane for a Dead Princess,* it was called. She didn't know what a pavane was, and she wasn't about to ask now. But the Dead Princess—how terrible. Was Tolyukov thinking maybe of a dead countess? She looked at him. His eyes were closed.

The music swept on, wave after wave. It was dreadfully sad, and very pretty. Erikka closed her eyes and leaned back.

After that one, there was something short and modern, loud and jarring with clicking sounds like coins being shaken in a glass jar. Erikka thought it was funny, and Francisco did, too. The old lady behind them disagreed. "Harold, I will not clap for such nonsense!" she said through the applause, and folded her arms determinedly. "It's an insult to any educated ear."

The third piece began, and suddenly Erikka felt sick.

A rush of pain in her stomach, a sudden dizziness and emptiness in her head. If I throw up here, Harold will have me tossed out on the street. She whispered to Tolyukov that she was going to the restroom, and then she tried to get out. People's knees and umbrellas and pocketbooks kept thrusting themselves in her path; the music was shrill, strident; people were coughing, and her head swam. Finally she reached the end of the row, and she ran up the aisle toward the lobby, trailing a length of white shawl behind her like a ghostly shadow.

When she felt a little better, she washed her face and looked at herself in the mirror. Pale. Very pale.

A couple of women had come into the restroom, and were talking to each other excitedly. Erikka's weakness and sickness suddenly left her when she recognized one of the voices. It was Mrs. Pruitt.

Erikka turned away from them and glided into the nearest cubicle. She knew she had not been seen, and she didn't want to be seen. Mrs. Pruitt was the last person in the world she felt up to facing at the moment.

"Regina, darling, what a sensible idea! To use the ladies' room just before the intermission and so avoid the rush."

"Only common sense, Dolly," said Regina Pruitt.

Erikka stood still as stone. When Regina and Dolly returned to the sinks to wash their hands, Erikka listened closely, so she could tell all this to Simon. He'd never believe it.

"That second piece—trash!" said Dolly. "I could sit down at a piano and play such garbage—and I've never had a lesson in my life."

De gustibus non est disputandum, thought Erikka.

"Well," said Dolly, "give me a good book any day."

"Me too," said Regina. "Dolly Frinkle, I've got the most wonderful prospect . . ."

"Oh, do tell," said Dolly.

"I couldn't," said Regina. "It isn't definite."

"Whisper."

"But really, I oughtn't."

"Just a hint."

Oh, brother, thought Erikka. Get on with it.

"Well," said Regina Hexler Pruitt, "Browler and I

have come across an autographed volume of *Leaves of Grass.*"

Dolly was saying nothing. Erikka could just picture the look on her face. Her double chin must be almost to her waist, her mouth wide open in astonishment.

"Do you *own* it?" asked Dolly, her voice an octave lower than normal.

"Very nearly. By next week, Dolly. I'll have you and Eustace in for sherry and you can see it. It'll be the crowning achievement of our collection."

"But where? Who? I hadn't heard of a Whitman being available," complained Dolly, her envy evident.

"The careful collector learns to keep an eye at every keyhole," said Regina. Erikka could not but agree. The worm. The repulsive worm! Erikka wanted to burst through the door and shove Mrs. Pruitt through the nearest available keyhole, but she controlled herself.

"I cannot disclose my source," Regina was saying. "It will not be an easy acquisition."

"Oh, you fox," said Dolly. "Do you mean skulduggery?"

"Sweet, scrupulous skulduggery," said Regina, and they burst into laughter.

Sounds of applause came from the hall.

"Thank you, thank you," said Regina playfully.

"Encore! You clever woman!" Dolly clapped.

Erikka threw up.

The two women, having forgotten that anyone else was

present, were suddenly silenced. Other women began coming in. Everything was noise and nausea.

"There's the little charmer," said the old lady to Harold when Erikka returned to her seat between Francisco de Medina and Mr. Tolyukov. "So glad she's not going to miss the big number."

"Are you okay?" said Francisco worriedly.

"Fine," said Erikka weakly, and turned to her right. "Mr. Tolyukov, have you decided to sell your volume of Whitman?"

"I'd rather die," answered Tolyukov.

"What's skulduggery?"

"Trickery. Sneakiness. Something underhanded and wrong."

"Shhh!" said the people around them.

"It's time for John Deaconson!" said the old lady behind them. "Oh, Harold, I can hardly stand it!"

The pianist came on stage. The audience greeted him with great energy. But Erikka sat, her head thrown back, eyes closed, thinking, thinking.

Chapter Nine

DREAM FEVER

"I know I oughtn't have let her go," said Mrs. Knorr, shaking the thermometer briskly. "But one hates to say no to everything . . . Erikka, now open your eyes. Open your eyes. I'm going to put this under your tongue and leave it there for a couple of minutes."

Erikka opened her eyes. Why did her mother's voice sound so loud? And what was everyone doing here in her room—all these bodies sticking up like so many oddly shaped cacti, around which the light from the ceiling's bare bulb splintered, to confuse her, to hurt her eyes.

She felt the thermometer slide into her mouth.

Do you want me to run out to a drugstore to get anything, Sharon? No, Kristina, let's wait a minute and see what's what. She moaned all night, Mommy; I would have come got you but I kept falling asleep every time I thought of it. Now don't worry, girls, it's just a fever, I'm sure. Martha Wong has a fever, Mommy, look at the fever in my mouth! Come here, Martha Wong, come see your Aunt Kristina.

Noisy cactus shapes, thought Erikka.

The thermometer slid out of her mouth and crashed to the floor.

"Oh, drat!" said Mrs. Knorr. Erikka opened her eyes again. Annie began to cry because without a thermometer Erikka would just have to stay sick forever.

"Everybody out," said Mrs. Knorr. "Maybe, Kristina, if you wouldn't mind dashing to the pharmacy . . ."

The ice-cold palm had left the brow, the second thermometer had slickly come and gone. The painful light had disappeared at last, and the door was closed. The noisy shapes were gone. With every passing minute, the blissful dark came up from the floor like waves of warm water, quietly, soothingly, higher and higher.

Erikka was wrapped in the heat of her fever.

She is in a forest, standing in the center of a spinney of birches. Everything shines green: the sun through the spring leaves, the shimmering spring air, the rustling grasses.

Erikka's inner voice sings to her:

All alone, all alone,
And these trees are my bones,
And these leaves are my skin,
And I'm all safe within.
All within me is mine
And my mind is my own,
All alone, all alone. All alone.

But of course she isn't. Here comes a cat, stepping by the spinney with great purpose and style. Countess Olga, twitching her whiskers in a fashionable way.

"Good day, Erikka Knorr," the Countess purrs.

"Good day, Your Countessness," says Erikka, managing a curtsey as best she can between the trunks of the birch trees.

"You haven't seen Tolyukov?" the Countess asks idly.

"Not so much as a whisker," Erikka says, proud of her wit.

"Could be he's gone," the Countess surmises intelligently. "And I in such terrible need. Oh, dear."

"Can I help you, Your Countess-ship?" Erikka asks politely.

"The moon grows fuller, Erikka!" says the Countess pointedly. And then she sits down to wait.

Erikka amuses herself, twining the green branches overhead to make a mint-green canopy through which the sun may greenly shine.

"Ahem," says a voice from beyond.

She looks out. It is Francisco, holding a violin.

"Play me a tune!" Erikka calls.

"Your request is my command," says Francisco grandly. *"Pavane for a Dead Princess.* Only make it happy."

Francisco says, "But I need a bow. Mrs. Pruitt took mine as last month's rent."

Erikka reaches up and snaps off part of her canopy. "Can you use it with the leaves still on it?" she asks worriedly.

"It's the best way," Francisco assures her. He takes the branch in his right hand and begins to play. The notes come rolling off the leaves like drops of water after a storm. They gather in little piles in the grass. Every so often the Countess bats a pile with her paw, and the notes ripple and strike each other pleasantly.

Francisco stops.

"The moon grows fuller, Erikka!" he says, and sits down in the emerald-green grass, through which the light runs, glistening.

Erikka isn't listening any more. She sees something coming from far away. She hears a noise like drumming.

It is Martha Wong, coming to the rescue on Toby! Martha Wong with a book bag full of thermometers! She screams "Whoa!" and Toby stops just by Erikka's little group of trees.

"Eat green grass!" says Martha Wong.

The Countess and Francisco and Erikka all begin to pull up grass from the cucumber-colored meadow.

"Not us," says Martha Wong. "Toby. We've got better!" She shows them how to use the thermometers like toothpicks, stabbing a musical note like a green olive in a drink and gulping it down. They make little musical gulps in their throats.

Suddenly Erikka realizes that she is on her hands and knees in the meadow greenness, seven or eight feet from her private private home.

"See, it's not so bad," says the Countess, popping three notes into her mouth and swallowing a lovely triplet.

"But one thing more," says Martha Wong. She stands her full imposing two-feet-five-inches and looks at Erikka critically. "The moon grows fuller, Erikka Knorr!"

And then, in a wink, the Countess and Francisco and Martha Wong and Toby are all gone. Erikka is left alone in the center of a close grove of birches.

The green slowly runs out of the day, through holes in the ground, and heavier dark descends, through holes in the sky. Erikka begins to feel hot and oppressed. She waits for the moon to rise, but it doesn't. Instead, the lines of the peeling bark of the birches reassemble themselves on the trunks of the trees, so that they look like eyes, single eyes, silver Cyclops eyes in a dark dark world, watching her unblinkingly. Erikka wants someone—she wants her mother to come, come and save her, come and close these eyes . . .

"Mommy!" she screams.

Mrs. Knorr was suddenly there, holding Erikka, placing a cold washcloth on her forehead, talking in calm, sensible sentences: nothing cryptic, nothing frightening. Erikka slowly dropped off into a deep, dreamless sleep.

Chapter Ten

UNDER THE
HALF MOON

The door opened.

Erikka heard it and turned her head to see. It was Bengt, his brown eyes large and solemn. "Rikka no sick!" he said authoritatively.

"I'm better," said Erikka.

Bengt relaxed. He scrabbled up on Inga's cot, over it to Annie's, over Annie's, and dropped in the space between Annie's cot and Erikka's bed. In his hand he had the pieces of a cookie he had brought as a present. He put them on Erikka's pillow and smiled.

"Play cars?" he said hopefully.

"Not just now," said Erikka. "I still feel tired."

"Mommy! Erikka said she's," yelled Bengt, beginning the laborious journey to the door. He was red with exertion and the importance of being a news bearer. "Tired. Rikka TIRED, Mommy." He disappeared.

Erikka closed her eyes again and smiled. What had her dream been about? Being in a sunny meadow in Russia, with someone . . . was it Aunt Kristina? She couldn't remember.

Oh, yes. The cat, and Annie and Francisco.

Erikka suddenly sat up. Her skin wrinkled with a dizzying realization.

Mrs. Knorr had piled the folded laundry on Erikka's dresser. The painting was hidden.

In one athletic lunge Erikka leaped from the bed and swept the laundry away. The watercolor mountainside was there, leaning against the wall, so vivid and simple it still made her gasp.

But now she stared for a different reason. The moon in the painting was not a slivery crescent as it had been. *It was a half moon.* It was white and looked like the sliced-off end of a hard-boiled egg. Erikka reached to touch it—but of course it was only a painting, only marks of water and pigment on a sheet of paper. The candle wasn't lit.

Maybe it's a sign, thought Erikka. That I should go back there. Tonight.

"Oh, you're up! And I am glad to see that." Mrs. Knorr came into the room. "How do you feel?"

"Okay," said Erikka. "A little wobbly."

"Well, you had quite a fever. Now, put on your bathrobe and come have some supper."

"Supper?"

Mrs. Knorr turned. "Erikka, it's Saturday evening. Don't you remember? You came home from the symphony last night very groggy and slept all day with a fever. You can come and have some tea now, and maybe some toast. Then it's right back to bed with you."

Erikka had other ideas about that.

* * *

But somehow the tea and the toast and the talking at the kitchen table made Erikka tired. She went into her room after supper and decided to lie down for just a minute. After Inga and Annie had gone to bed, she would get up and light the candle and go back to the mountain . . .

When Erikka awoke on Sunday morning and realized that she had slept clear through the night, missing her chance to go into the picture, she was furious with herself. And for a while she was furious with everyone else, too, refusing to say goodbye as her mother and Inga ran off to church, refusing to play with Annie and Bengt under the kitchen table, refusing the comics that Aunt Kristina offered her. She picked up a pencil by the telephone and started doodling on the edge of the newspaper (which was something that Mrs. Knorr got angry about, because she saved all the papers for Mr. Knorr to skim through on his weekends home).

Erikka was drawing moons, dozens of moons, from the slimmest crescent blooming to the perfect circle and back again, when something caught her eye. A word had flashed out at her, something she recognized, and she couldn't find it again. So she started at the top, reading every item and line.

Halfway down the page, she read:

Last night Chicago blue bloods Browler and Regina Hexler Pruitt entertained in royal fashion at the Pearlman Plaza. Seventy-five of Chicago's finest were on hand to celebrate what the Pruitts claimed was their thirtieth year of befriending the Arts. "The record speaks for itself," said Art Institute Director Elliot Boering in his after-dinner address. "The Pruitts' generosity has enabled thousands of the less fortunate to enjoy the cultural treasures Chicago has to offer. Their donations to symphony, dance, museums, and galleries have insured that Chicagoans will continue to enjoy the benefits of the Fine Arts for years to come." Dinner included an avocado salad, vichyssoise, Veal Oscar—

"What's a blue blood?" asked Erikka.

"Someone who comes from a long and distinguished line," said Kristina, deep in the editorials.

"A long and distinguished line of what?"

"People." Kristina put her paper down for a minute. "It's your family history, it's what your family is. Social prominence, or noble blood. If your ancestors are important, or wealthy and well known."

"But the Pruitts aren't related to any kings."

Aunt Kristina read the article quickly.

"Well, America doesn't have any noble families, of course. Sometimes American blue bloods are people who are directly descended from families who came over from England and took part in the American Revolution. Or else people with inherited money. They're no better than you or I, of course."

"Then why does it sound like they're so great?"

"These particular people happen to have money. They are moneyed. Or so it sounds. They seem to be very philanthropic—"

"What's that?"

"Generous, concerned for the good of their fellow human beings."

"Hah!" said Erikka loudly.

"Hah! Hah!" chorused Annie and Bengt, from under the table.

"You sound as if you know them," said Aunt Kristina.

"Only too well," said Erikka darkly, enjoying herself. "I've run into them here and there. Am I a blue blood?"

"Not by their standards. Your parents both came from Sweden in the past twenty years, and so did I. I don't know much about your new mother's background. But most people don't put too much value in this any more, Erikka. You are what you make of yourself. And you are a good girl."

"A good girl. Thanks," said Erikka. "A good girl who never gets to eat avocado salad and Veal Oscar and whatever that other thing is. I wouldn't know what an avocado was if one fell right out of the sky on me."

"Well! I'm not good for much but I can remedy that problem." Aunt Kristina flapped the paper open and disappeared behind it. "I'll take a walk after I get dressed and find some avocados for lunch."

* * *

Mrs. Knorr took off her good Sunday coat, revealing the usual flannel shirt underneath. Erikka grimaced inside; her teeth ground against each other and her tongue curled up to the top of her mouth. Why couldn't she wear a dress on Sunday?

"So how do you feel?" Mrs. Knorr palmed Erikka's forehead.

"I don't know. How do I feel?"

"You feel normal. I guess it was a quick bug. But you'd best take it easy for a few days." Mrs. Knorr hung up her coat.

Aunt Kristina came in a minute later. "Oh, you're home. I got some fixings for lunch, a salad."

"That was nice of you, but not necessary," said Mrs. Knorr, squaring away the papers and not noticing (or ignoring) the page Erikka had doodled on. "But there's plenty here for salad. We've lettuce and tomato and some dressing—"

"I promised Erikka I'd buy some avocados. As a special present."

Mrs. Knorr continued piling the papers, but she moved more slowly, not looking at Aunt Kristina. "Avocados! Aren't you luxurious, Kristina. We usually stick to lettuce and tomato."

"Well just for a change," said Kristina quickly.

"Don't develop a taste for them, Erikka, or you'll have to get a job to support your habits." Mrs. Knorr deposited the papers in the living room. "Avocados, really."

She came back into the kitchen. "And mushrooms too."
Kristina, this is elegant fare for the thrifty Knorr family."

Aunt Kristina took off her coat. Her white blouse
caught the sun like the sail of a boat skimming over Lake
Michigan. "I'll fix lunch today," she said to Mrs. Knorr.
"You sit down and rest. I'm glad for the chance to do
something for you."

"I'd be foolish to pass up this opportunity," said Mrs.
Knorr. She sat down next to Erikka. It made Erikka feel
awkward, as if they were sitting together on a bus and
didn't know what to say to each other. She had never seen
her mother just sitting before.

"Do you need some help?" asked Erikka, bouncing up
from her chair, eager to break this funny feeling.

"Can you slice mushrooms?" asked Aunt Kristina.

"I'll try."

"Nice weather for this time of year," said Mrs. Knorr,
in a voice that sounded like someone else.

"It is. I've been lucky on this trip. I hope my next week
here in Chicago is as nice," said Kristina, deftly pulling
away the skins of the avocados with a knife.

Erikka gave her mother a sidelong glance. She looked
nervous.

"Here, Mommy, will you do this?" she said, and thrust
the mushrooms and the cutting board across the table at
her.

"Certainly," said Mrs. Knorr, reaching for them eagerly.
Her hands moved like clockwork, reducing the mush-

rooms to stacks of perfect slices in minutes. She looked more like herself. Erikka breathed easier.

"Mushrooms," muttered Mrs. Knorr happily to herself.

"What does Chicago look like from the plane?" Erikka asked her aunt.

"We flew in over the lake. The buildings rose up suddenly, frightfully high and close to the lakeshore, like guardian towers of some dark land. It's strange, descending into the Chicago haze. Everything is the color of newspapers, gray and dirty white."

"Now, Kristina, don't you think flying is exciting?" said Mrs. Knorr.

"Oh, it is," agreed Kristina. She continued chopping the green avocados into a bowl.

"And Chicago is beautiful, in its own way," said Mrs. Knorr. "Right here I can find examples of the work of almost every important modern architect, and examples of every trend and innovation in urban architectural style from the past hundred years." Erikka grimaced.

The doorbell rang. Annie ran to get it. Bengt followed.

"What's for lunch?" asked Inga, passing through the kitchen on her way to check the front door.

"Avocado salad!" said Erikka in an enthusiastic way.

"Yuck," said Inga, as Erikka had known she would.

"It's your friend," said Annie, returning to the kitchen and skidding to a stop underneath the table.

"Whose? Whose?" asked Inga and Erikka quickly.

"Go see," ordered Annie.

Inga ran, and returned a minute later with Simon Cameron, who was grinning sheepishly.

"Everyone's sick as dogs over there, so I'm free," he said. "I thought I'd take advantage of the surprise vacation and come see where you lived."

"Oh," said Erikka. "Well. Meet my Aunt Kristina. She's making some avocado salad. And this is Inga, my younger sister—"

"Younger but smarter," said Inga, helping herself to a mushroom.

"Hands out of that," said Mrs. Knorr, swatting Inga away.

"And this is my mother. And Annie is under the table. And Bengt is somewhere off in the front room," said Erikka breathlessly.

"Hello," said Mrs. Knorr. "What's your name?"

"Oh, sorry," said Erikka. "Simon Cameron. You remember."

"Yes," said Mrs. Knorr. "Will you have lunch with us, Simon? You can call your mother if you like. The phone's there on the wall."

"Hanging by a nail," said Inga. "It came out of the plaster one day."

"I've always wondered how that happened," said Mrs. Knorr, fixing a stern eye on Inga.

"I am entirely innocent," said Inga. "Go on, Simon, call."

"Inga!" said Erikka, turning red.

"What?"

"I don't have a mother," said Simon.

"Oh. Well, that's no big thing. I don't know why Erikka is so upset. We didn't have a mother for a while, either."

"Have you a father?" said Mrs. Knorr.

"MOMMY!" said Erikka. "Really!"

"Either he has or he hasn't, Erikka, nothing to be so fainthearted about."

"Yes, but I don't live with him. I live at a school," said Simon. He sat down without being asked, but Erikka didn't think anyone minded.

"Time for lunch," called Kristina. Bengt came running.

"I want peanut butter," said Annie.

"So do I," said Bengt.

"You know what this avado looks like," said Inga.

"AVOCADO," said Erikka loudly.

"Avocado. It looks like cut-up sections of the Formica tabletop in the school cafeteria, doesn't it, Erikka?"

"Lovely salad, Kristina," said Mrs. Knorr.

"Did you ever have avocado salad at a party?" Erikka asked her mother.

"No." Mrs. Knorr paused. "The last party I went to, I dressed to the hilt and embarrassed myself and your father."

"How?" said Inga.

"Inga!" said Erikka.

"Stop being so bossy," shouted Inga. "I can say what I want."

"Enough, lambs," said Mrs. Knorr mildly. "You know

I never drink. Your father and I went to a party given by his boss. It was in a new house in Evanston, built with all the current dramatic touches—glass walls, custom-built furniture, and a cantilevered deck that hung out over a garden. Nice, in a way. Well, the boss's wife was showing the wives around the house, pointing to all the objets d'art and acting as if they were really nothing at all, and in the bedroom I fell over the platform the bed was raised up on. I just didn't see it, and I fell right on my hands and knees."

"So? How is that embarrassing?" asked Inga. Simon was just watching like crazy.

"Well, that was bad enough. It looked as if I had had too much to drink. But then we went back to the front room, and the only chair left was this low white one. I sat in it—it was very soft—and I sank, and sank, and sank, till my knees were almost up to my chin. And I sat there and *knew* I was going to have to be pulled out. I'd never be able to manage it by myself unless I rolled the whole chair over and crawled out from underneath it. So when dinner was announced, I struggled and pushed and finally had to call your father. He came and pulled me out, in full view of the rest of the guests, who were waiting in the dining room. They were all gracious, but I could tell they thought I was drunk. The whole idea of it made me laugh myself, which only made things worse. The impression I made was somewhat less than respectable."

Aunt Kristina and Simon laughed and laughed. Inga and Erikka and Annie all looked at each other.

"Well. I don't think that's so funny," said Erikka coldly. "Making a spectacle of yourself."

Mrs. Knorr was laughing now, too. "I couldn't help it, Erikka. And it was funny. I don't ever care if I go to another party there."

"Do you go to parties, Aunt Kristina?" asked Erikka, to change the subject.

"Oh, yes, all the time," said Aunt Kristina, and then, "Well, now and then. I had something of the same sort happen to me at a party in Rome last year—"

"Rome! Like with the Pope?" asked Inga.

"The same Rome," said Kristina. "I was there on business."

"Have you ever been to Rome, Mommy?" asked Inga.

"No, darling, I've never been. The farthest east I've gone is New York City."

"What did you do there?"

"Gave a paper at a national conference on the methods of construction used for the Chartres Cathedral. A good paper it was, too, though I suppose of limited interest to the general public."

"Oh, really?" Erikka was interested. "How was it?"

"The conference itself was fascinating, and well worth the trip. New York, architecturally speaking, was like a buffet: bits and pieces of everything all jammed together. The buildings I enjoyed. I was only mildly impressed with the city on the whole. Too big. Ever been to New York, Simon?"

"No," said Simon. It was the only thing he said through the whole meal.

Erikka was embarrassed at her mother again, saying that New York City was only mildly impressive. "Don't you like anything?" she said sullenly.

"I like a class of intelligent students and I like a cup of coffee and I like my children around me," said Mrs. Knorr in a singsong way. "It takes all kinds to make a world, Erikka. I wouldn't mind traveling off to Rome in Aunt Kristina's shoes sometimes . . . in fact, I've given more than a little thought to the idea of a sabbatical in France sometime in the next few years. That would require, of course, our sticking to franks and beans for a while. In the meantime, the floors need to be swept and the bills to be paid, and the majestic history of architecture to be passed on to new students. And that's what I'm doing. I bet Aunt Kristina wishes she could have four children as nice as mine."

"Sometimes I do," said Kristina.

Really, thought Erikka, this is getting worse by the minute. I don't believe it, anyway; who in their right mind would give up travel and prestige such as Aunt Kristina has to be the mother of four kids in a crummy apartment in Chicago, Illinois?

"I want to go to Rome," insisted Erikka.

"Wherever you wander, wherever you roam," said Mrs. Knorr.

"Be it ever so humble, there's no place like home," they all finished; only Erikka didn't swallow it, not for a minute.

After lunch and dishes, Erikka said she would walk Simon to the corner. Mrs. Knorr told Simon to come again soon; Inga and Annie echoed their mother's sentiments with smiles. Aunt Kristina said *"Au revoir!"* in a wonderful worldly way, and Bengt paid no attention to any of them, crawling into the cabinet where the pots and pans were kept.

Erikka and Simon took long steps, carefully avoiding sidewalk cracks and conversation, till they reached the corner. Then Erikka said, "So now you've seen the absolute truth about my family. Hard to take, isn't it?"

"Oh, I don't know," said Simon. "I kind of liked them."

"Well, try *living* with them. Almost impossible. And they never like anything that's really *worth* anything—except Aunt Kristina, and she's different."

"They seemed perfectly nice to me," said Simon, swinging around a street light. "In fact, they were nothing like what I thought they'd be from the way you described them."

"You're just being polite because you had lunch there. They're tiring and maddening. Didn't you hear cranky Inga making fun of Annie because she spilt her milk? Or my mother saying *New York City* was *boring?* I was so embarrassed. It's a real trial sometimes."

"I think you're a real trial sometimes," said Simon, without malice. "So what if your mother said New York

City was boring? I thought you hated cities, too."

"I do, but *New York City* is different," said Erikka stubbornly.

"You've never even been there. You're just cranky for the fun of it."

"I am not."

"I mean, look: you're always griping and moaning and saying someone else is terrible. You're on everyone's back all the time. I didn't head *you* say anything so startling or wonderful at lunch. In fact, you were right at home with them, arguing and being crabby and everything. You aren't so charming yourself."

"I never said I was charming!" Erikka looked heatedly at him. "And so what if I argued with them. They start it. They live on arguing. It's their daily bread. I'm more like Aunt Kristina."

"And she's nice enough."

"I know what you mean." Erikka felt her anger slowly being absorbed by a humiliating self-pity. She was reddening, and the threat of tears made her voice husky. "She's nice but I'm not. She's all traveling and glamorous, and I'm a clunky, boring, twelve-year-old girl who is stuck with hair the color of cardboard and no talent at anything at all."

"I didn't say that," said Simon. "It's just that you always complain about everybody else but you're kind of a crank yourself. I don't mean that as an insult," he added.

"Then thanks for the compliment. Very thoughtful, after you've just had lunch at my house."

"Don't get all huffy."

"According to you, that's all I get is huffy."

Simon got mad. "Well, you do. Even in those crazy stories you tell me about the old witch in the woods—you're complaining about her and calling her names and wishing she was somewhere else. Like that whole stupid mountain is just for you. All you ever think about is yourself. If those stories you tell really are true, I bet you've made that old witch feel just terrible. I bet she just—"

"You don't know anything about feeling terrible!" And here Erikka burst into tears.

"Are you kidding?" said Simon, right through her tears, right to her face. "Where I live, I don't know anything about feeling terrible? Give me a break." He started to walk away.

Then he turned and called out, "It's you who don't know anything about feeling good, when you have everything to feel good about."

And finally he yelled, "And thanks for lunch."

Erikka went home, drying her eyes with the ends of her long, ordinary hair.

That evening, when the house was quiet and her sisters asleep, Erikka crept out of bed and found the matches in her bottom dresser drawer. Simon's horrid accusations still ringing in her ears—were they true?—she lit the candle in the old ornate candlestick. She noticed that the candle was growing shorter, even as the moon was growing fuller . . .

Grasping the heavy thing in her hands, she moved forward. Once again the dark of the bedroom and the dark of the woods became one, and she was the only spot of light, penetrating the woods, the branches, the inexplicable density of the transition; and then she was through, out onto the hillside, underneath the half moon that shone cold and white as ice.

There was no one waiting to greet her.

Odd, she thought.

She walked slowly into the clearing, being careful to shield the flame from any sudden wind. But tonight, as before, the night was generously calm. The stars in their fastenings twirled, the light from moon and stars spilled luxuriously in the clearing. The warm scent of the Adirondacks in April wafted around her like incense.

She was afraid to set the candle down, on a rock or a level space, in case the wind should come up and extinguish the flame. "The fires of the sanctuary must not be dimmed," she whispered to herself. Or else she might not get back.

So she sat down at the edge of the cliff, and she could see the rich dark color of the lake in the valley below, and she held the candlestick in her lap, and she was alone.

She kicked her legs.

She threw a pine cone over the edge of the cliff, to see how far down the drop was. A dark shape like a tattered rag disengaged itself from a tree and drifted over her. An owl.

She whistled for a minute.

She thought about being the daughter of the moon, in love with all good things, and all the good things were stretched out before her like the riches of a king's treasury: the slumbering hills, the secret lake, the distant stars, the silent moon, the private night.

And then Erikka thought: Well, perhaps I should go see Theresa, just to make sure she's all right. After all, she's so old.

You're just thinking that because Simon said you were a crab, she told herself, not moving. Simon said that maybe Theresa felt terrible because of your selfish crabby griping. You don't have to do something just because Simon says. You're not playing Simon Says, anyway!

She smiled, for a second.

But the joke didn't last. The night was so rich and powerful that it soaked things up out of Erikka: her defensiveness, her stubbornness. She sat at the edge of the cliff, shivering a little, but without someone to share it with, the far-flung sky seemed remote and desolate.

Maybe he was right, she thought. Well, suppose for a minute he was. About Theresa, at least. Here you are, miraculously introduced to an old woman, through some inexplicable magic. Unhappy as you are, still you're here, and maybe you're the only person old Theresa has. Is that why you've been given this fierce magic? To come befriend an old woman?

You can't paint yet, she said to herself sternly. You

can't move out of Chicago. You can't even get along with your family. Maybe the least you can do is go see old witch Theresa and try to be decent.

And, this decided, she leaped up.

Her muscles were so delighted with something to do that she arrived at the cabin before she'd even thought of what to say. A light gleamed dimly through the glass. She knocked. A voice told her to come in.

Theresa Maloy sat on a stool near the fireplace, with her chin in one hand. She barely glanced over at Erikka.

"Hello," said the girl.

Theresa pointed to one of the chairs. Erikka set down the candlestick, and sat, and relaxed her limbs by the fire. For a long time she watched the flames doing their endless dance along the logs. Then a sound from Theresa caught her attention.

Theresa was crying, clutching her shawl to her face, turning her wide old eyes down to her lap. Erikka didn't know what to do. She jumped out of her chair and went to Theresa. Instinctively she put her arms around her, and rocked her slowly, patting the back of her head as if she were a child like Annie, crooning and cooing as if she were rocking a baby to sleep. Even as she did this, Erikka couldn't help thinking: What am I doing? I have never done this before, except to Bengt or Annie. I have never had to comfort an adult before. How do I know what to do? But she did.

She led the old woman to a bench where they could

both sit, and she wrapped the blanket around Theresa's narrow shoulders and said nothing. Erikka took the old hands into hers and rubbed them softly, feeling the knobs, the wrinkles, almost feeling the blood feebly coursing through. Slowly Theresa's sobs died down.

Finally Theresa shook her head and dried her eyes with the palms of her hands—just as Annie or Bengt would, thought Erikka. And then she set her old eyes looking at Erikka.

"What's the matter?" asked Erikka.

"You are so young," said Theresa, "and you tell me you want to be alone, and I am so old and so alone. And you leave me in anger."

"Oh," said Erikka.

"You think people are for turning away from. You think they are like diseases to be caught. And you turn away from me."

"But I came back, see?" said Erikka, feeling guilty and terrible.

"You don't know loneliness, you are too much a child. You have no heart."

"I have all the heart I can stand," said Erikka, hearing echoes of Simon's words in this and feeling uncomfortable.

"You have no heart. You turn from me and run off in the shadows. You tell me you would rather I were not here. You want to be alone with your heartless self." Theresa said these lines solemnly, like a litany. "You turn away from my tea. You turn away from my necklace.

Even if you are a ghost, you are a terrible one."

"I am not a ghost."

"You turn away from other ghosts."

"Will you *stop* it. Look, I came to see you tonight, didn't I? I hugged you when you were crying."

"You couldn't help it. You didn't know what else to do." Theresa looked away. "Shall we have some tea while we argue the state of your heart?"

"You sit down. I'll make it. Dry your eyes." Erikka grunted, lifting the heavy kettle to its hook over the fire. "I came because I wanted to see you. I was sorry I was so mean. I was upset that night. Where're the tea leaves?"

"In the tin canister. On that shelf. No, to the right, next to the dead philodendron. Why are you upset that night?"

"Long story. I was mad at my mother. My stepmother, really. And I guess I was mad at you, too. I'm sorry." Erikka stood in the middle of the floor, her hands clutching at her hem. "Really, I *am* sorry. I didn't mean to make you cry. That's a bad thing to do. Please accept my apologies."

"Well." Theresa sniffed.

"There's so much I want to do myself," said Erikka slowly, "and I can't do it yet. Not paint, or live where I want, or anything. Maybe it makes me mean sometimes— but it's not on purpose, honest."

The old woman pointed. "The water's boiling, daughter. Put some fresh leaves in the pot, and when it's steeped, pour the cups half full and add more hot water from the kettle. That's the way I've always made tea . . ."

"And I do love people," said Erikka, spooning tea leaves into the pot, dropping some dark flakes into the fire. "I love some good friends. And I love my family, sort of, only not in a way to shout about."

"My family is all dead," said Theresa from her bench. She nodded emphatically. "Every one, burned in a fire, except me. I am out at a dinner party that night, and come home to an inferno on the lawn. The servants, and the old father, and my family all."

"Oh, no." Erikka sat down again next to Theresa.

"Roasted like potatoes."

"Stop," said Erikka.

"Well, it is so long ago. I can be honest about it. And so I live alone." Her eyes moved around the room and settled on something on the center table. Was she looking at the candlestick?

"And these days are filled with ghosts, or the memories of ghosts," she said, almost to herself.

"Don't you see people at all?" Erikka brought over a cup of tea.

"I go into the village for supplies. I don't need much. I don't see many people. Few know I'm here even, though I am fifteen years in this same cabin."

"Is this land yours?"

"No. Not a square inch of it, nor this little house, either. I just live here because it is empty. It belongs to a family down by the lake. I rent it for a small sum—I never see them. Only their son comes walking here in the woods, on this mountain, sometimes. I live alone, I live apart from my family and beloved, across uncrossable reaches. And so it is a surprise to have company." Theresa smiled uncertainly. "And a delight."

"Some delight, when I've been such an idiot," said Erikka. "I am glad to see you."

"Then I give you my necklace as a gift. It is old and is my mother's." Theresa struggled to her feet and found the necklace on a hook near her bed. "I have no children. This is for you, daughter."

Erikka bowed her head gratefully as the necklace went on. Theresa arranged it carefully. It lay heavy and cold against her nightgown. "Thank you."

The old woman sat down again, and rocked, and purred. Erikka fingered the necklace, its bright stones and filligreed settings, and she was silent. And she was glad to be with someone.

Theresa was lost in thought. She stared at the candle-stick as if trying to memorize each loop of wax, each protrusion of gold, each bead and oval and diamond of design in the bright surface. Erikka turned to look at it, too, standing in the center of the table, for all the world like a candle on an altar, which it once had been . . .

Suddenly she let out a sound and rushed across the room.

"The candle's burned down so far!" she said. "I've got to go back before it burns out entirely!"

Theresa leaped up. "Well, come quickly, daughter," she

said. "We have not time to waste."

"You don't have to come," began Erikka.

"Nonsense. I—I—" and here she sneezed.

"You'll catch cold. Stay here. I'll come back in a night or two," said Erikka firmly. And Theresa suddenly nodded assent.

"Just hurry," pleaded the old woman. "Don't get caught here. There is no end of trouble if you do." And then she sneezed again.

"God bless you," said Erikka, hugging her quickly.

"And God speed to you, daughter," said Theresa.

I am becoming quite the mountain girl, thought Erikka, pleased with herself. She raced over the path to the clearing which was her doorstep back into her bedroom. Her feet were sure, her hands tight on the candlestick and protective of its flame. The moon in the sky was like a sentinel, curious, friendly, alert, the light from its half-opened eye following her, keeping her way visible and easy.

When she reached the pine tree she knew best, the one whose branches were the foreground in her aunt's painting, she turned for a moment.

"Oh, if this is a dream, let me remember it as long as I live," she cried aloud.

And then she wheeled about and pitched herself into the edges of the tree, in the direction from where she always came, and at the same time she puffed the candle out.

Tipping and twisting through the dark thickness, she came slowly into her own bedroom, where Annie and Inga were sleeping.

She set the candlestick reverently down on the dresser and saw that there was less than an inch of wax left to burn. It would have to be saved for the very last trip.

And Erikka went to sleep and had no dreams.

Chapter Eleven

CROCODILES
ON THE LOOSE

The next morning Annie was sick. It was the same thing, fever and a head cold and exhaustion, so Mrs. Knorr spent breakfast time at her bedside. Erikka fed Bengt, who was annoyed at the disruption of the daily schedule. "Annie no sick!" He pounded his spoon on the table. Erikka gave him another piece of toast to keep him quiet, and thought quickly. If she was careful, she could manage to slip out to school before her mother realized that she really ought to stay home for another couple of days. And there was no need of that—Erikka felt just fine. Besides, she wanted to go see Tolyukov in the afternoon. There were so few days left. This was Monday, and he would be moving on Saturday.

Inga was kind enough to get Erikka's books from her dresser, so that Erikka wouldn't have to go in the bedroom and run the risk of being told to stay home. And then Inga and Erikka raced off to school.

When three o'clock finally came, Erikka ducked out of the back door of the school and across the back parking lot. This was against the rules, but it was a quicker way to Simon's school.

As usual, Simon had somehow known she would be coming today, and he was ready, having already sneaked out at the end of *his* last class. "I'm getting quite good at it. I bet I spend more time away from the prison than anyone else on my level."

"Pride goeth before a fall," rattled Erikka automatically, and then: "You're being nice to me. I should be apologizing for being so cranky yesterday."

"No, I should apologize," said Simon, "for being rude."

"Well, our apologies cancel each other out, so let's forget them. I have to tell you something. When you came yesterday, I was so preoccupied with my family I forgot to tell you about the night at the symphony." And Erikka told him about Mrs. Pruitt in the ladies' room.

"A real spy," said Simon in an admiring tone. "Good work."

"And then last night I saw old Theresa Maloy again," continued Erikka.

"You're not still going on about that old lady?" asked Simon. "Come on, Erikka. Enough is enough."

"*Why* will you refuse to believe me?" said Erikka, more incredulous than angry. "I've never lied to you, Simon. I'm not one for making up stories and pretending they're real! Just because this is outside the limits of your experience—"

"Stop sounding like a teacher," said Simon. "What proof do I have? Sure I trust you, Erikka. But this is wild. If I told you that I had suddenly been left a million dollars in a will, would you believe me?"

"Yes. Instantly."

"You would not," said Simon.

Erikka took her books and started swiftly down the street. "You are a real puzzle to me, Simon Cameron," she said. "I can't tell why we're friends, since we don't seem to be able to communicate with each other."

They walked in obdurate silence, looking opposite ways, till they reached the bookstore.

The CLOSED sign was in the window. Erikka rapped on the front door. There was no answer.

"We could go around in the alley," she said. "I went out that door once. Maybe Tolyukov is so busy working in his back room that he can't hear us."

Past bedsprings and garbage cans and an old rusting car that had part of a tree opening its buds through the space where the glass ought to be, Simon and Erikka picked their way. "Look at that fat cat in the alley," said Erikka, pointing. "She's twice as big as the Countess."

"Probably eats fat rats in the alley," said Simon, and Erikka ran to the back door, squealing.

The back door was open.

"Mr. Tolyukov?" called Erikka, peering in over the mountain of boxes.

The Countess came gliding to the door and rubbed up against Erikka's legs, mewing with unusual vigor.

"I think something's wrong," said Erikka. "Oh, Simon. Do you think that Tolyukov—that he might be—"

"Let's see," said Simon grimly. He stepped in the back

door. Erikka picked up the Countess, stroking her, soothing her, and followed.

There were no bodies on the floor, in the back room or in the bookstore proper. But the place had been torn apart. All the books that they had neatly piled in boxes were strewn on the floor. The painted chest was open and its bundles scattered around. Erikka saw her precious blue vase on the floor, rolled up against the baseboard. It wasn't broken. She rushed over to it.

Simon came back from the bookstore section. "A regular mess."

"Let's start cleaning up," suggested Erikka.

"But we ought to call the police. We oughtn't to touch anything. They might be able to get a clue," protested Simon.

"Think how Mr. Tolyukov is going to feel." Erikka righted the overturned rocker. "The less of a shock this is, the better. Besides, we know what is gone and who took it."

Simon simply stared at her.

"The book. Tolyukov will come home and find that his volume of poetry has been stolen. Mrs. Pruitt—or someone working for her—has stolen it. It's as plain as day." Erikka sounded as if she was going to cry. "So come on. Let's try to make this a little less catastrophic."

"Are you going to tell Mr. Tolyukov that you know who took it?"

Erikka didn't know.

* * *

Fifteen minutes later, Tolyukov let himself in the bookstore entrance. Simon and Erikka called out hellos immediately, so he wouldn't be frightened. He had a bag of groceries with him.

"What's this?" he asked. Erikka told him how they had come in the back door, and how they'd found the back room a disaster.

"My book," said Tolyukov. "My poems."

He went straight to the painted chest in the back room, ignoring the mess and the upheaval. He searched through the piles of mementos and boxes. He sat back on his heels. He did not look too upset.

"I suppose," he said, "when it is time for one thing to end, it is time for many things to end."

They watched him.

"Well, pull me up, Erikka. I suppose this has happened for a reason. I was awfully fond of that book—fond of the words in it, the sentiment, fond of the signature and of my ownership. I suppose that I can always buy a paperback copy if I want to hear those poems again."

"Aren't you going to call the police?" asked Simon.

"No. Oh, I suppose I should: a thief shouldn't get away with his thieving. But being that I'm leaving this store, and being that the book was so valuable to me—well, I guess it teaches me a lesson."

Erikka was silent. You don't need to learn that lesson, she thought.

Tolyukov settled in his rocker. For a minute or two he rocked, rubbing the hair on the Countess' neck. "And it is not all lost," he mused. "If the book has been valuable to me, it is a value that remains after the book has gone, I suppose . . . 'A man is a summons and challenge . . .'"

"It's time to go," said Simon.

Erikka got up. Suddenly she said, "Mr. Tolyukov, do you know how to get to the medical college where Francisco is studying? I want to see him today."

Tolyukov gave directions. It wasn't far.

"It's only four o'clock now," said Erikka. "Can you come with me to find Francisco?"

"If we hurry. Why didn't you tell Tolyukov that you knew Mrs. Pruitt had stolen the book?"

"Don't you think he can figure that out himself? She's the only one—besides us—who even knows he had it. No, if he's not going to stand and fight her, *we* have to, Simon. And you can see he's not going to battle. He's folding up right in front of our eyes. So it's our job. We've been completely unable to make her pay her bill—and that was partly our fault. We won't mess it up this time, Simon! We'll get it back! I swear it! We have one week. It won't do Tolyukov any good financially, since he won't sell the thing. But it is *his*. It is his treasure. And I know how much a treasure means to someone."

"But why are we looking for Francisco?"

"Well." Erikka looked thoughtful. "I kept my mouth shut about Mrs. Pruitt and her evil plans when we were at

Tolyukov's. I think if I had told him that I knew she had stolen it, he would only have said that it didn't matter. He is worn out. But I think it is time to get someone's help. And Francisco likes Mr. Tolyukov. He might be able to think of something."

"He might not believe you."

"Wait and see."

The secretary at the reception desk seemed a little surprised when Erikka said she had to find Francisco de Medina. "But if he's a first-year student, he's in a class right now," she said nervously.

"It's an emergency," said Simon.

"Of epic proportions," added Erikka.

"Well . . . he's in Lecture Hall 108. But I don't think you ought to disturb the class."

"Thank you," said Erikka.

They found the double doors to Lecture Hall 108. They both took deep breaths and then Erikka pulled the right-hand door open.

The room was deep and white; the students' desks were arranged on descending platforms; the teacher's podium was far beneath them. They were at the very back of the room, and at the top; it was like coming into a very steeply sloping movie theater. No one even turned to stare at them. The room was crackling with fierce energy. The students scribbled frantically on wildly flapping notebook pages—there was Francisco, as thoroughly absorbed in reams of notes as the rest—and the teacher was having fun at the board, drawing diagrams in four colors of chalk.

Erikka and Simon found two seats at the very back of the room, where they had come in. When they realized no one was going to rush at them and throw them out, they relaxed a bit and looked around. "It's a bunch of mad scientists," said Simon. "Francisco's not mad," Erikka whispered back. "Shhh."

"Excessive constriction of systematic blood vessels leads to ischemia and cerebral hypoxia," said the teacher. "As the brain cells starve for oxygen, one develops confusion, disorientation, and failure of memory. Thus, senility."

"Are you saying, Doctor, that the administration of nicotinic acid is successful therapy?" asked the student.

"Combined with a high potency multivitamin supplement. Any other questions?"

"Does it hurt to have your head cut off?" Simon whispered to Erikka.

"Be sure to tune in next time, for the Glory of Vitamin B-12," said the doctor.

Books slammed, voices murmured, legs stretched. The lecture was over. Francisco closed his notebook and looked around the room, as if he had just come out of a dream that was more intense than any of his waking hours. He almost fell out of the chair when he saw Erikka and Simon at the top of the room.

When he reached them, he said, "Well, what did you think?"

"Brilliant," said Simon, grinning. "Just brilliant."

"The doctor or the spotlights?" asked Francisco.

"I don't understand," said Erikka.

"You ought to have raised your hand and asked a question," said Simon.

"No—what I don't understand is how you can be doing this," said Erikka to Francisco. "What we heard was so confusing, so scientific. Yuck. So inhuman."

"Oh, but it is human, it's all about taking care of humans," said Francisco.

"It seems like dead facts. How can you stand it? How can you be a musician and play beautiful sounds in a beautiful way, and then all day long talk about all these long words and stuff? How can you be a romantic musician and a brainy doctor at the same time?" Erikka sounded very distraught.

Francisco put his books down on the desk. The room was nearly empty, except for the doctor, who was answering a question in the front of the room, and some students. Francisco pretended to pick up a violin and tune it and adjust the tension of an imaginary bow.

"Listen," he said.

"Chaconne in D minor," he said.

His arm leaped up; the imaginary bow came down on the imaginary strings. Fingers worked, picking out the imaginary tones; foot tapped, keeping exact time. Really, thought Erikka, I can almost hear it.

After a minute, Francisco stopped. "If you take a piece

of music," he said, "you can cut it up into any number of parts. Take the Chaconne in D minor. Put it on the operating table." Francisco hurriedly laid down his imaginary violin (carefully, so it wouldn't fall on the floor), and then stretched out a length of imaginary music on an imaginary operating table. "Now. We have our instruments. Scalpel. Tweezers. Fascia slasher. Tuning fork. Let's see: here we have"—he carefully lifted something out with the imaginary tweezers—"a string of quarter notes! Let's hang them here, on the edge of the desk. And here, a restated melody. Here's a couple of eighth-note rests. Here's the theme: thick, bold, obvious. But it looks like nothing when we take it out of context."

Erikka and Simon watched, mesmerized. So did the doctor and a few straggling students who had come up behind Francisco very quietly.

"See this crescendo marking?" asked Francisco, holding nothing up to the light. "Alone, it looks useless. Just two long lines hitched together at the end. But if we put it back in the body, it *does* something. It gives direction. It provides information. It is a part, Erikka, of a whole. If you love the whole thing, then you love the parts it's made up of. And you learn about them. And the learning is exciting."

"Hear, hear," said the doctor, behind them. "Mr. de Medina, I applaud your observations." Francisco whirled around, astonished. "Don't let me interrupt the lecture and demonstration," said the doctor kindly. "Just be sure to clean up these key signatures before you leave."

"Erikka," said Simon, "it's getting late."

"The matter at hand," said Erikka. "Francisco, we need your help."

She told him what had happened, both at the symphony the other evening and at the bookstore that afternoon. Francisco sat down on a desk and listened without speaking.

"What are you proposing?" he asked, when Erikka had finished.

"We don't know," she said unhappily. "We were hoping you could think of something. And fast."

"If Tolyukov accepts this theft without any complaint, do you think he'd really want us to try to see justice done?" asked Francisco. "In other words, is it any of our business?"

"Yes, it is," said Erikka. And Simon agreed.

"Maybe I could go see Mrs. Pruitt and hint that there is evidence that she's behind it all," murmured Francisco. "Maybe I could scare her into giving it back. Maybe I could bargain with her."

Erikka held her breath.

"But what if she didn't take it?" Francisco suddenly asked. "What if someone just happened to find it, as they were pawing about the bookstore looking for things to steal?"

"I don't believe it," said Erikka. "I'm sure it was her."

"Let me think about it," decided Francisco. "I'll be home from school tomorrow about four. Come and see me, and

I'll try to come up with something."

Erikka and Simon looked at each other. It was the best they could do.

"I've got lab in fifteen minutes," said Francisco. "Do you want a soda? Or do you want to look around?"

"No," said Simon. "I have to get going."

"Me too," Erikka agreed. "But thanks for explaining how you can study all these facts and stuff and still be a musician. I didn't understand it at all, but your explanation was nice."

When Erikka got home for supper, her mother had already gone to work. Once again, Florry from downstairs was not coming to mind them, because Aunt Kristina was still visiting.

At the kitchen table, the Three Terrors were diminished to two. Annie was still sick. She had spent the whole day in bed.

"Poor dear," said Aunt Kristina, passing around the sandwiches. "Your mother didn't want to leave her tonight, but what could she do? I promised to call her if anything happened."

"Is Annie *that* sick?" asked Erikka with a start.

"No. It's just a cold. But your mother is so concerned."

"She was having funny dreams this afternoon, Mommy said," Inga told Erikka. "At one point, she started screaming that there was a crocodile under her bed. Mommy went in to calm her and asked her how she knew. She said, 'Because he told me.' And then she went right back to sleep."

"Annie SICK!" said Bengt.

"I think there are a lot of crocodiles on the loose," said Erikka darkly. "Inga, eat your crusts."

"You can't make me," said Inga. "You're not the boss."

Chapter Twelve

HOUSEBOUND

"When are you going home, Aunt Kristina?" asked Inga when they were doing the dishes.

"That's a rude question," said Erikka, snapping the dish towel at her sister's neck.

Inga turned and blew some suds at Erikka. "It's not because I *want* her to leave, you dummy. I just wondered."

"This weekend," said Aunt Kristina. "My business meetings ought to be finished by Friday, and then I'll try to catch a flight back to Boston on Saturday, I think. I'm hoping to get a chance to look in at the Art Institute some afternoon before I go. Maybe you two could meet me downtown and we could have dinner together?"

Inga scrubbed the silverware enthusiastically. "That'd be *great*, Aunt Kristina."

"Just think! We could sit in a booth, maybe," said Erikka.

Bengt got up from his place under the kitchen table and hurried out to the front room to look for his tractor. Aunt Kristina stirred the soup she was making for Annie's supper. "Do you like the Renoirs at the Art Institute?" Erikka asked her.

"Oh, yes, and the landscapes and the sculpture," said Aunt Kristina. "My new book is going to have lots of watercolor landscapes in it."

"Hmm. Renoir," said Inga thoughtfully, as if she knew his work well.

"You couldn't tell a Renoir from the Sunday comics," Erikka reminded her.

"Don't squabble," said Aunt Kristina mildly. This was such a surprise that they both turned to her, and she looked at them.

"We weren't *squabbling*," said Inga.

"We were only *talking*," said Erikka.

"Do you want to hear real squabbling?" Inga asked. "We'd be happy to demonstrate."

"No, no." Aunt Kristina threw her hands up in defense. "I guess I've forgotten what it's like to be sisters. Since your mother died, I've been alone in my family. You Knorr children are my only blood relatives. And anyway, your mother was so much older than I that I always treated her as a grownup when I was small."

"Were you sad when she died?" asked Erikka.

"Of course I was, Erikka. Heartbroken. And I miss her more than I— Oh, look! I've burned the soup." Kristina moved a pot. "How can you burn soup?"

"You cook it too long at a too high temperature," said Inga.

Bengt came running into the kitchen. "Snowing! Snowing!" he shouted.

"No. Not in April, not in the last week of April." Aunt Kristina ladled out the soup that wasn't too burned. Erikka and Inga leaned up close to the kitchen window and looked out. They could see the brick wall of the next building, which was almost close enough to touch (if they had climbed on the sink and opened the window). And Bengt was right. In the narrow alley, snow was falling heavily.

"I can't believe it," said Erikka.

When the others were in bed, Erikka and Aunt Kristina sat in the living room. Erikka was embarrassed as usual about the rip in the sofa where the stuffing was coming out, so she sat there to hide it. Aunt Kristina had taken out the paints she had given Erikka, to demonstrate them again—those beautiful watercolors, in little bottles with eyedroppers in them, all bright colors, iridescent treasures —and paper and a brush. She filled up the plastic dish basin with water and carried it into the living room and set it down on some newspapers. And then she spread out her paper, thick white paper that felt as heavy as starched linen.

"Why do you have so much water?" asked Erikka.

"The more I have, the less often I have to change it," said Aunt Kristina. "It gets dirty very quickly."

"It's really a wild snowstorm." Erikka gazed out the front window.

"I hope your mother doesn't get caught in it. How far away does she work?"

"I don't know. I think she has to take the el, though."

Aunt Kristina dipped in her paintbrush and shook some of the water off onto a thick pile of old newspapers. She was kneeling on the floor, and the paper was before her, white, empty, capable of bearing whatever images Aunt Kristina chose. She must feel like God, to be able to make things out of almost nothing!

Aunt Kristina held her paintbrush up, to see how much water was in it. With a sudden chill, Erikka saw the shape of the wet bristles, and it was the same shape as the flame of a candle . . .

And then red. Red like the red of stained glass. And yellow, as piercingly yellow as yellow could possibly be without becoming something altogether new. Erikka watched in amazement as the colors ran together, like the voices of two instruments harmonizing, a thread of orange, a ribbon of orange, and then a road of orange. It was a red hill and an orange road and a yellow sky! And then Aunt Kristina flicked the paper aside and started something else. The whole thing had taken about ten seconds.

There weren't even any words to say. Erikka turned away, staring at the ugly pattern of wallpaper, wishing and wishing that someday she would be capable of doing something so beautiful.

It almost seemed too sacred to watch. Aunt Kristina had forgotten for a moment that anyone else was there. With her brush like liquid light, she poured colors onto the white pages, softly talking to herself, dismayed over this and throwing it aside, elated about this and leaning back to see it from a distance. Erikka turned and looked out the window again. In the glare of the street light she saw the snow swirling. She watched it. Start, stall, thicken, slacken, stop. Start again.

She moved closer to the window, forgetting for a minute about the stuffing in the sofa. This was really a storm. Merriam Street—what little of it she could see—was under attack by the fiercest of enemies. All the little details of things were disappearing: the cracks in the sidewalks, the lines of mortar between bricks, the words on store signs. The air was thick with white. Like thousands of sheets of white paper, Erikka thought, descending from the sky.

Aunt Kristina had paused. "Erikka, now I've demonstrated. You try."

"Oh, no, I can't."

"Yes, of course you can. They're your paints. Come on."

Erikka knelt down nervously. She twisted her hair up on her neck and stared at the paper. Its whiteness threatened her, seemed to mirror her own emptiness and inability. "I don't know what to paint."

"Just play with the colors. Experiment. Relax!"

Erikka dipped her brush into the color called cyclamen. It was a pinkish rosy-red, and she tried to outline a rose on the page. But the lines were too thick—it looked like a lollipop such as Annie might draw—and Erikka angrily xxx'd it out and said, "I'd rather watch you. You know how."

Aunt Kristina said, "You must be patient, Erikka."

I've been waiting, thought Erikka, for a very long time.

Kristina continued, "I have a question for you."

"What?"

"I would like to get your mother something, in exchange for being responsible for the vase being broken. Do you have any suggestions?"

"No," said Erikka. "It's a nice idea, Aunt Kristina, but I don't. I think she'd be just as happy with a piece of beef for a stew as with anything else."

"She wouldn't be interested in one of my paintings, I suppose," said Aunt Kristina, almost to herself.

"She's not interested in art." Erikka tried not to sound condescending.

"I don't think it's that," said Kristina distractedly. "She's got other important matters to tend to."

Erikka wasn't sure what Kristina meant.

Inga came out into the front room.

"I know, I know, I'm supposed to be in bed," she said, anticipating Erikka's remarks. "But have you seen how hard it's snowing? It's piled up three inches since dinnertime! I measured it with a ruler on the ledge of the bathroom window."

Erikka was disappointed that Inga had interrupted the conversation, but she followed her to the front window. Aunt Kristina came up behind them.

The street look like a white canyon. Winds tore great gusts of snow from one end to the other. "It's going to be a big storm, is my guess," said Inga.

"Look, girls." Aunt Kristina pointed.

At the end of Merriam Street they could see a dark form. A person, bent almost double, struggling against the wind. Making slow progress up the middle of the street.

"It's Mommy. I'll make some hot chocolate," said Inga.

"I'll clear away this mess," said Aunt Kristina, and in one swoop she had gathered the paintings, the wonderful paintings, and had crumpled them up like trash!

"You've ruined them!" said Erikka.

"They were only sketches, just cartoons," said Aunt Kristina. "Here, could you carry this water and dump it in the sink?"

When Mrs. Knorr arrived, Erikka and Inga and Aunt Kristina were waiting for her. "Hot chocolate! That's a treat. I'll overlook the fact that both you girls should be in bed by this hour," said Mrs. Knorr, taking off her husband's old parka and shaking the snow from her hair. "I had to wait for forty-five minutes for the train. This snow is surprising everyone. Look, Erikka, Inga, I brought you both a present." From under her jacket Mrs. Knorr drew out a paper bag. "The main office has invested in some new equipment; I found these in the trash. You can use them for your school work if you want." She brought forth two staplers. "Only don't ask me to buy you staples when these run out. You'll have to use your allowance money if you want more."

"Sit down, Mommy, drink your hot chocolate," said Inga.

"In a minute. First I want to go see how Annie is." Mrs. Knorr left the room.

"Do you see what I mean?" said Aunt Kristina quietly.

Erikka felt funny. All she could think of were the watercolors, all wrinkled and ruined in the kitchen trash. Maybe she could straighten them out.

There was no chance of meeting Francisco on Tuesday the way she had planned to. There was no chance of meeting anyone.

"Where do you think you're going?" Mrs. Knorr had asked when Erikka arrived at the breakfast table dressed in her school clothes.

Erikka had said sinkingly, "No school?" and then gone to change her clothes.

It was still snowing. The house was dark because the snow had fallen on the windows and the wind had died down so it didn't blow away. "I think we'll just have to resign ourselves to a day or two in the house," said Mrs. Knorr. "This storm has crippled Chicago."

"How can we have a storm in April?" said Erikka crossly. "There's not supposed to be snow after Easter. I thought that was a rule."

"She's mad because she's going to miss out on art class," said Inga.

"Why does it have to snow?" Erikka kicked the table.

" 'Though the mills of God grind slowly, yet they grind exceeding small,' " quoted Inga righteously.

"They do not. Shut up. Besides, you don't even know

what that means. You just got it out of the literature book that your baby grade reads," said Erikka.

"Well, you don't know what it means, either, you jerk."

"Now we're squabbling," Erikka informed Aunt Kristina as she leaned over and broke the yolk in Inga's poached egg.

"Erikka, stop your nonsense," said Mrs. Knorr sharply. "Go get Bengt up, will you, and change his diaper right away. I can see this is going to be a pleasant confinement."

Aunt Kristina said, "I called my boss. He said not to try to get in today; that he was the only one who made it to the office, and he was going to turn around and go right home."

Annie came to the kitchen door, rubbing her neck and looking as if she had been in a fight with a bear. "I want breakfast," she said, and went over and climbed up on Mrs. Knorr's lap.

"Annie, don't eat all the Cheerios, I want some," called Erikka from the bathroom.

"I'm not Annie, I'm MARTHA WONG," screamed Annie, shaking her head in outrage. "And besides, I will eat all the Cheerios if I want to."

"Happy days are here again," said Mrs. Knorr, jiggling Annie up and down on her lap.

"This is the stupidest snowstorm I have ever had the privilege to see," said Erikka at lunchtime.

"Can we go out after lunch, Mommy, and take Bengt

for a ride on the Flexible Flyer?"

"I'm afraid not, Inga. There's been too much sickness going around. Tomorrow will be time enough."

"But we might have school tomorrow."

"You won't. It's still coming down, look at it. And it isn't slated to let up till some time late this evening. Now you might as well relax."

"Stupid idiot," muttered Inga, under her breath.

"What was that, Inga? I'd watch my step if I were you," said Mrs. Knorr.

"Perhaps we could play a game this afternoon," said Aunt Kristina.

"When my *real* mother was alive, I didn't have to stay in the house in a snowstorm," said Inga.

"Enough, Inga," said Mrs. Knorr in one of those voices.

"You want to call up your friend Carmela and see if she can come over, Inga?" said Erikka quickly.

"Stupid rules. Always stupid rules," said Inga, slurping her soup on purpose.

"Too much. Be so kind as to go to your room, Inga Katrinka Knorr," said Mrs. Knorr. "More soup, Kristina?"

"Well, I don't care," said Inga loudly. She got up and pounded down the hall to the bedroom where Aunt Kristina was staying.

"Not that room—go into Erikka's," called Mrs. Knorr calmly.

"I don't even have my own room!" yelled Inga from her distance. She went into Erikka's room and tried to slam the door, but Toby was in the way.

Aunt Kristina looked embarrassed.

"Don't mind her, Kristina," said Mrs. Knorr, getting up to locate some dessert. "I'm sure she's just catching the same bug that the others had."

"I didn't have a bug," said Annie.

"You did, too," teased Erikka.

"Where?" said Annie sullenly.

"No bugs on Annie!" said Aunt Kristina, and pulled Annie onto her lap. Annie smiled.

"I hope you stay here forever and ever," Annie said, playing with the earrings Kristina wore. "Are you going to?"

"I doubt it, sweetie," said Aunt Kristina.

Bengt slid down out of the high chair and took his place on Aunt Kristina's other knee. Erikka got up and helped her mother clear off the table.

After lunch, the apartment became quiet. Aunt Kristina was writing some letters in Inga's bedroom. Annie and Bengt were taking naps: that is, Bengt was sleeping in the crib in Mrs. Knorr's bedroom and Annie was trying on some of Erikka's clothes in Erikka's bedroom. Inga had fallen asleep.

Mrs. Knorr got out some mending and took it into the front room. Erikka, bored, followed her there.

"Mommy, I'm supposed to meet somebody at four o'clock today," she said, just in case her mother had had a change of heart.

"Who?"

"Francisco de Medina. The med student who lives next to the bookstore."

"What on earth for?"

"Well, it's a long story."

"Do you want to tell me?"

"No."

There was a silence while Mrs. Knorr selected the white thread and quickly shot it through the eye of the needle, a task which took Erikka at least half an hour and usually left her in tears.

"Can I go to meet him?"

"No."

"If I tell you why, will you let me go?"

"No."

Erikka sighed.

"It's a blizzard, Erikka, a spring blizzard. There's nothing moving. No sidewalks are shoveled. And that bookstore is five or six blocks, over on Ingoldsby Street, isn't it?"

"Yes."

"Well, that's too far, for whatever reason. Maybe tomorrow, if things seem a little beter."

Erikka stretched out on the couch.

"Shoes off the sofa, Erikka."

"Why?"

"You tell me."

"Because my shoes are dirty."

"Smart girl." Mrs. Knorr held up an old school blouse

of Erikka's and matched the rip in the collar with a piece of white material from something else.

"I don't know why you care about this couch," said Erikka moodily. "It's in terrible shape."

"It's the only one we have," said Mrs. Knorr.

"It's got stuffing coming out!" Erikka pulled the wadding even further, so her mother could see it. "Look at this! How can you stand it?"

"I didn't know it was that bad."

"Well, it is. Why don't we get a new couch?"

"Why don't we move to Palm Beach?"

"Answer me, Mommy!"

"You tell me."

"Oh." Erikka hated to have to answer these "You tell me" questions. "Because we can't afford it, probably."

"Smart girl."

"Why can't we afford anything decent?"

"Erikka!" Mrs. Knorr seemed surprised. "You are warm and well-fed. You go to a good school."

"Why don't we buy a new couch? Why don't we eat avocados?"

"It's a matter of priorities. There are still some hospital bills to be paid. We're not swamped in debt, but your father and I are both frugal. And what I said about going abroad to do some further study was not just idle talk. We'll omit the avocados in favor of other benefits."

"Why don't we at least get a slipcover or something?"

"Why don't you take a needle and thread right now and see if you can make it a little more presentable," suggested

Mrs. Knorr, "since you seem to have nothing better to do at the moment."

"That's not what I meant," said Erikka, but she came over to her mother's basket and found a nice thick needle and some strong thread.

"When is Daddy coming home?"

"Well, I don't know. If they get this storm all the way across the plains, he might be a little late. I expect him this weekend."

Erikka jabbed the needle into the thick maroon upholstery. It was harder than it looked.

"Do you like being married?" Erikka asked.

"Yes."

"But Daddy is hardly ever home."

"I know. I wish he were home more often. Maybe someday he'll get a promotion to dispatcher and be able to be home all the time."

"Did you know he was going to be on the road almost all the time when you married him?"

"Yes."

"Then why did you?"

Mrs. Knorr put down her sewing for a minute. "Because I wanted to, Erikka."

"It doesn't make sense to me," said Erikka.

"What doesn't make sense?"

"All you've got are four kids who aren't even your own. And Daddy is only home every other weekend. That doesn't strike me as such a bargain."

Mrs. Knorr smiled, despite herself.

"Four little pests," said Erikka.

"Now, *really,* Erikka!"

"Well . . . Three Terrors and me."

"You're being silly today. Did I tell you that I got a letter from my brother Bruce? You have a new cousin. His daughter Sarah had a baby."

"Boy or girl?"

"Boy. I'm not sure what they're going to call him."

"I never knew I would have cousins from you. All I know are the cousins from Daddy's family."

"But of course you do! Not many, to be sure. You have an aunt and an uncle and a couple of cousins. If you look in that box of photographs in the bookcase, you can see pictures of your Uncle Bruce and Aunt Marion. They came to the wedding."

Erikka soon returned with the box. Large glossy pictures slid out onto her lap. One was a portrait of her father and second mother taken on the church steps.

"Why aren't you in your wedding gown?"

"Erikka, you remember. I didn't wear a wedding gown. I wore that nice gray suit."

Somehow, Erikka hadn't remembered. She could still picture the long dusty church and the way the small number of guests only filled up the first four pews, and the way her father had looked, tall and neater than ever before. But she couldn't remember what Mrs. Knorr had looked like.

"No white dress," she said. "But that's terrible. How could you?"

"It wasn't appropriate," said Mrs. Knorr. "Your first mother had been dead only a while. There was no need for a lot of show. It would have been disrespectful."

"How could you stand it? *All* weddings are supposed to have brides in white, with long veils and flowers and ladies in colored dresses. I see them coming out of St. Mary's almost every Saturday morning."

"I had flowers," said Mrs. Knorr. "You can probably see them there. They were a little bouquet of some white flower. So you see, there was white in it."

Erikka stared at the picture. It all seemed immensely sad.

"See, there's your Aunt Marion, and next to her is my brother, your Uncle Bruce. Do you remember him? And there's Aunt Kristina. And there's a picture of you and Inga, and Annie crying in the stroller."

"Where was Bengt?"

"Florry was minding him for the day."

"I'll bet he's sorry he wasn't there."

"He'll never remember it. You remember it, don't you?"

"Not much. I get it mixed up with our first mother's funeral, because both times there were a lot of people there that I didn't know."

Mrs. Knorr put down the blouse and picked up a pair of pants that Annie had worn the knees out of. Erikka put down the photographs and went back to trying to make the couch a little less awful.

* * *

It lasted all day; it didn't peter out till the evening. On Wednesday everything was still closed and dead. Inga didn't care any more because she was sick and was generally miserable, anyway. But Erikka was furious, and disappointed, too. She had wanted to help Tolyukov with more of his packing. She had wanted to get back to Francisco to see if he had come up with an idea for getting back that stolen book. She had wanted to see Simon, even though he never believed her any more about anything.

At least on Wednesday she was able to clear a path from the front door to the deli. Florry was glad to see her. She gave her a whole big package of sliced ham, wrapped up in white paper and string, as a present for the family. "Business is so lousy," she said. "It's good to see a friendly face, doll."

Erikka thought of the friendly faces she wanted to see as she carried the ham upstairs. Oh, family was fine for a couple of days, but there were other things to worry about now.

Tomorrow she would get out, for sure.

Chapter Thirteen

THE ONLY
IDEA LEFT

On Thursday, things were not much better, but Mrs. Knorr had had about as much as she could take. Annie and Bengt were bundled up carefully, scarves and boots and mittens that didn't match, and they were sent out to play in the snow. Erikka was appointed protector.

She was as thrilled as the little ones to be out. Merriam Street had finally been cleared, and great mountains of snow lined the street, fifteen feet high where the plow had piled them. Because all the cars had been plowed in, people were strolling arm in arm down the center of Merriam Street, as if it were the fairway in a carnival. Merchants, shoveling out their doorways, grumbled good-naturedly to each other about the business they'd lost due to the storm. Erikka and Bengt and Annie scaled the snowbank nearest their house. They were so high they could almost see in their own front windows, where Inga was watching and waving.

"Poor Inga," said Annie, throwing a handful of snow at her. "Too bad she's so sick."

"We ought to get her a present," said Erikka.

"Yes," said Annie. Bengt was too busy falling off the snowhill to answer.

"What do you think?" asked Erikka, rescuing Bengt.

"A snowman!" suggested Annie gleefully, jumping on top of Erikka and knocking her down.

"No," said Erikka. "I know a nice store. Maybe we can get her a nice book in a bookstore I know."

"Okay," said Annie. Bengt didn't care.

A student who had an apartment across the street from the Knorrs had put two stereo loudspeakers in the window and was broadcasting some triumphal horn music out over the street. People smiled. None of the kids from the other end of the street even tried to knock the speakers off the ledge with snowballs, which Erikka thought was unusually public-spirited of them.

Simon suddenly came in sight, loping down the middle of the street. He grinned and shouted when he saw Erikka. She jumped down into the street. "What are you doing out in the middle of the day?" she said.

"You'd never believe it. Most of our teachers are either sick or couldn't show up because of the snow, so they made us go out in the back field to play. Well, Jeff Murray sneaked out, and then Kevin Steptoe, and then everyone in the whole section left! One by one, out the part of the fence where there's a loose iron rail. We're all going to get creamed for sure when we go back. But I thought I might as well enjoy my day out." He threw some snow up in the air; it came down into his curls. Annie laughed in her calculated fetching manner.

Erikka said, "Well, there's a lot to be done. We've got to go see Francisco; this has been the first chance I've had."

"Who's *that* one?" asked Annie, tugging at Erikka's scarf and surveying Simon with undisguised interest.

"You remember. That's my good friend Simon Cameron," said Erikka, picking Annie up and kissing her.

"Don't kiss me. You have bugs," said Annie.

Then Bengt clamored to be picked up, too. So Erikka handed Annie over to Simon (Annie was far more delighted with this arrangement than Simon), and they started off down the middle of the street toward Tolyukov's bookstore.

Ingoldsby Street was as much of a mess as Merriam and the rest of Chicago. When the four children reached the bookstore, they were all panting from the effort of wading through unshoveled lawns and climbing to the pinnacles of newborn Himalayas and leaping from snow cliff to snow cliff.

Tolyukov was just going out. "To the bank. To explain that I'm closing my business."

"Oh, those Pruitts," said Erikka fiercely.

"Oh, save your wrath," said Tolyukov, locking the bookstore door and waving to the Countess, who sat, bored, in the window. "The Pruitts are going to pay their bill. They're coming on Saturday with a check; they called and told me so. But it doesn't make any difference. They're taking their business elsewhere—and without their business or a broader financial foundation, I can't hope to survive. Someone's coming tomorrow to take away the boxes I spent all weekend packing—and the rest is going back to the publishers. It's surprising how quickly you can adjust to these changes, Erikka. And I'm adjusting. So don't blame the Pruitts. They're not responsible for my getting so old. And they're not lawless."

"They *are* lawless," said Erikka as Tolyukov disappeared around a corner. "Thieves and criminals."

"They're paying their bill," said Simon.

"They stole Tolyukov's book, and who wants them as customers, anyway?"

"Let's not argue. Listen—I can hear Francisco sawing away on his violin."

Erikka and Simon looked up. They could see the windows of what had to be Francisco's rooms—but the snow was plowed mercilessly right up against his front door. Even if they could tunnel for the doorbell, Francisco could never manage to get the door open.

But Erikka said, "Isn't there a staircase by Tolyukov's back door? There must be one at Francisco's house, too."

They forged through the drifts in the alley to the back door. Annie and Bengt were no longer interested in this expedition, so Erika said they could play in the alley. Annie started climbing a bedspring that was propped up against a side wall, and Bengt stared adoringly at her.

"Who?" said a fat woman who came to the door when they had pounded on it quite a while.

"Francisco de Medina. The violinist," said Erikka.

The woman wiped her hands on her apron. "Oh. The Mad Musician. How's a body to hear the TV with all that racket going on? I thank my stars he isn't here all day long *every* day. Second door at the top of the stairs. Use the railing—the stairs is steep."

Simon and Erikka squeezed past her and ran to the right-hand door on the second floor. Simon knocked.

The music stopped. Francisco opened the door. "Oh. It's you. Come on in!" he said.

They followed him into a neat white room with a table, and a mattress on the floor, and a music stand, and a large map of the world pinned to the wall.

"Practicing my Vivaldi," said Francisco. He put down the instrument lovingly and said, "How're things going?"

"We got stuck in the snow," said Erikka. She was itching to look around, to see what books were lined up against the wall, and to look at the postcards taped to the closet door. But this was business, so she kept her eyes trained on him. "Of course, today's the earliest I could come."

"And we're thinking about getting that book back from the Pruitts," said Francisco.

"And if we can blow them up in the bargain . . ." added Simon sweetly.

Francisco sat on the edge of his table and tapped his forehead with the tip of his bow. "I've had a hard time formulating any real plans, I have to admit," he said. "The best I've come up with is the thought that you ought to be SURE that the Pruitts actually have the book before you think about anything else. You could get in a lot of trouble even hinting that they stole it if they really didn't."

"I am CERTAIN, as certain as I am of day and night," said Erikka, clenching fists and gritting teeth in demonstration of inviolable certainty.

"Then it oughtn't to be too hard to find out. If Mrs. Pruitt was boasting to that other lady that she might obtain this book, then that's a pretty good sign that she'd consider it a feather in her cap to own it—"

"I'll rip every feather out of her cap," said Erikka.

"She hasn't got a feather for a brain," said Simon.

"She has the book," Francisco reminded them. "At least, she might. You've got to find out for sure. Someone whom she doesn't know should go and talk to her and pretend to have an overwhelming interest in her book collection. If she's as proud as she sounds, she might wheel out her latest finding on a silver platter. People sometimes let their pride get the best of them, you know."

"And pride goeth before a fall, so maybe she'll fall," said Simon.

"You might be right about Mrs. Pruitt's pride, Francisco," said Erikka admiringly. "How do you know so much about people?"

"I'm a med student. I study people," said Francisco, winking.

Annie and Bengt were both crying in the alley when Simon and Erikka returned. Bengt buried his face in

Erikka's knees. Annie scrambled up into Simon's arms.

"No present for Inga," said Erikka. "The store's closed."

They turned and made their way out to Ingoldsby Street. As in a summer storm, the streets ran with dirty water. Icicles dripped, roof gutters spouted silver ropes. Sewers gurgled. It was only natural, thought Erikka, splashing, being so late in the year. Being the end of April. Being two days till May. Being two days till Tolyukov left his bookstore. Erikka blinked back a tear. No time for that now.

"Francisco's idea might work," she said to Simon, shifting Bengt to her other hip. "If we can find out where the book is, maybe we can make concrete plans to put our hands on it."

"Are you and I going to go?" she asked him a minute later.

"Are you crazy? They'd know us a mile away. And how well could we convince them that we were in love with old books? It'll have to be someone else."

Erikka's heart fell. She hadn't thought of this.

"There's no one," she said.

"Don't be an idiot," said Simon. "What about your Aunt Kristina? She's so fond of you. And you're always saying how wonderful she is. Wouldn't she do this for you?"

Erikka blinked again in the strong sunlight flooding down Ingoldsby Street. "I don't know . . . she might."

"She'd better, because there's no one else," said Simon.

Chapter Fourteen

AUNT KRISTINA
IN THE ARENA

"There's no one else," Erikka finished.

Aunt Kristina put down her cup of coffee and looked at her niece. "What makes you think I could pull off such a crazy stunt?" she asked kindly.

"You know all about things," said Erikka, staring into her untouched bowl of Cheerios. "You've been all over the world. You're an artist."

"I'm not an actress."

"It wouldn't be acting for you, to be enthusiastic over old books, would it?" argued Erikka. "You have an artist's eye."

Aunt Kristina sat up straight and looked at the kitchen clock. Six o'clock in the morning. Erikka had woken her at five-thirty by tapping on the door, and had asked for special help. How could she refuse? This was Astrid's oldest daughter, sitting opposite her, whose eyes were cast down but whose hands tugged at each other nervously. She seemed so intense sometimes. She was like Astrid and Kristina herself, when they were girls back in Borgholm.

Every day there was something crucial. Every day something hung in the balance.

And it's true, thought Kristina. All the time, battles and crises. Maybe it's not as important to do this for Erikka's funny old man as it is to do it for Erikka. Maybe she's the one who needs the support now.

"I hear your mother getting up," said Kristina. "I'll call the Pruitts this morning and see what I can do."

"Thank you," said Erikka quietly. She poured milk into the bowl with wordless deliberateness. Sobriety could sometimes be as eloquent as ebullience.

After school Erikka darted over to the Dearborn School for Boys. There was no sign of Simon. The arrogant young man at the front desk refused to take a message, saying that all the boys in the fourth division were being punished. Erikka used her best emergency phrase and said that it was a crisis of epic proportions. The young man at the desk didn't care.

Aunt Kristina arrived home from the office at the same time Erikka came in from school.

"I've got to hurry," she said to Erikka, pulling off her coat even as she ran up the stairs to the Knorrs' apartment. "I'm supposed to have a glass of sherry with the Pruitts at four-thirty this afternoon."

Erikka followed her down the hall to the bedroom. "Can I come? And wait around the corner? I won't be in the way."

"Ask your mother," said Kristina, as she disappeared to change her clothes.

Mrs. Knorr was sufficiently busy with sorting laundry to give Erikka a distracted "Well, yes, if it's all right with your aunt." So Erikka raced down the hall to her own room, nearly crashing into Toby, whose rear parts still stuck out in the hall. She grabbed a handful of change for the el and then went and sat in the front room to wait for her aunt.

"I swear, I must be loony to be doing this," said Aunt Kristina, as they set out briskly down Merriam Street.

"What does loony mean?" Erikka struggled to keep up.

"Crazy. It's from that Latin word for moon, luna. Remember: 'Luna, every woman's friend'? In the old times, people thought that the moon was the cause of insanity. Its pull somehow became associated with craziness. Hence, someone affected by the moon, someone crazy, is loony."

"The moon!" Erikka stopped short. "Over by the edge of Martin's Drugs. It's full."

"So it is," said Kristina. "Come on. I'm afraid that I cut things a little too close." She found some change in her pocket and gave it to the lady collecting fares for the train. She and Erikka hurried up the steps to the platform.

Chicago stretched away from the rail of the platform like a backdrop for a play. Erikka caught her breath and leaned over the rail to look. Below, some kids were playing in the alleys behind Merriam Street. She could just barely see the corner of the gray building where the Knorrs lived. And Ingoldsby Street was out of view, hidden behind the tall stubborn old buildings that crowded the neighborhood.

"Look," said Kristina, pointing. Across the way an old, old woman was standing on a fire escape. She was lifting her cane and aiming it at the sky, yelling something to someone inside. After a minute, a large woman with two babies in her arms came out onto the fire escape. The wind lifted her apron and the sheets on the line; the birds on the roof fluttered up and down. The old lady was pointing out the moon to the younger woman, who looked at it for a moment, jostling the babies against her to keep them happy, and then went back in. The old woman put her cane down, but kept staring up at the white sphere, rising in the still-light sky.

"Smart old woman," said Kristina.

Erikka stared, and wondered how that old woman felt, living with a daughter and grandchildren in a crummy couple of rooms overlooking an alleyway and a gas station.

But she had the moon, and she knew it.

The train flew into the station, and Kristina and Erikka boarded. The old woman probably stands there every night before supper, Erikka thought, watching the sky.

"I mentioned that I was a friend of Dolly Frinkle's, the way you suggested," said Kristina, settling in the seat. "And that Dolly had recommended that I come to see the Pruitts' library of rare books. I told her that I was an artist

—which is true. And you're right, Erikka, I will be interested to see the books, and to see an autographed copy of Walt Whitman's poetry. I only hope that I can carry it off."

"You'll be fine," said Erikka, and she believed it, too.

Fifteen minutes. Twenty minutes. Erikka's heart felt like a mass of jelly; it seemed to be slipping around in her, making her have to swallow suddenly, making her almost lose her balance as she walked along the curb.

Well, things must be okay or Kristina would have been out right away. Erikka looked up at the tall apartment building on Lake Shore Drive, a pillar of glass and chrome reflecting the sunset.

Surely it couldn't hurt if she waited in the lobby? The Pruitts wouldn't be coming downstairs; there was no danger of being caught.

The next step, thought Erikka, as she moved inch by inch closer and closer to the front door of the apartment building, was going to be a difficult one. Aunt Kristina had said that it would be just as wrong to steal the book from the Pruitts as it was for the Pruitts to steal it in the first place (that is, providing they *were* the ones who had taken it). The best you can hope for, Aunt Kristina had said, is to make sure that they *do* have it, and then call the police. If you're going to try to steal it yourself, I can't help you.

Erikka wasn't sure if she agreed with this reasoning, but she had promised not to try to steal the book. And now she had to come up with the next step: when to call the police. When to have a raid on the Pruitts' apartment, to their complete shock and surprise, so they wouldn't have time to hide it. Obviously, it would have to be tonight. Oh, if only everything worked out right! If they could be caught red-handed! Tolyukov might then be able to persuade them to continue their patronage of his store! They would squirm—oh, it would be grand to see them squirm— but in the end, to save their reputations, they would give in and agree to do business again. And Tolyukov could reopen his store and everything would be perfect.

By now Erikka was standing, first on one foot and then on the other, in the lobby. She stared at the floor numbers over the elevator doors. No one was at the fifteenth floor, which was where the Pruitts' luxury apartment was.

It couldn't hurt, really it couldn't, to take the elevator to the fifteenth floor. She could wait in the little nook at the end of the hall; there had been a broom closet or something there. She would be sure to hear Aunt Kristina coming out.

"Fifteenth floor," she said to the elevator man, as calmly as she could, as if she *always* visited her good friends the Pruitts whenever she was in town.

The hall was empty. And quiet, fearfully quiet, as if no one at all was around. For a minute Erikka considered going up to the door and listening for conversation, but she knew that the Pruitts' living room was a distance away. And it was better not to press her luck.

She found her nook, just as she remembered it from the

time when she and Simon had come begging for mercy. The broom closet was locked. Bet the Pruitts have solid sterling-silver brooms! Erikka giggled despite the terrible gravity of the situation.

She almost fell on the floor when suddenly the door of the broom closet opened, from the inside.

There was no time to hide, or run, or anything. She just stood there in terror.

It was that fat woman, the Pruitts' maid.

"What're you doing here?" she asked, much less irascible than the last time.

"Uh . . . uh . . . I'm waiting for my aunt," said Erikka. She immediately could have kicked herself. That was a moment for a good lie. And she just hadn't been prepared.

"Is that the woman in with the Pruitts?" said the maid.

"Mmmmmmm," said Erikka, her brain racing. Should she suddenly dash for the elevator? Chances were the woman could follow her and pick her up in her big flabby arms and squeeze her to death before the elevator doors could open.

"Well, no need for you to wait out here," said the maid. "Come on in and have a glass of milk."

If Erikka refused, the woman might get angry and tell the Pruitts that there was a little vagrant in the hall. Oh, why hadn't she stayed around the corner where she was supposed to be?

With a feeling of doom she managed to push past the

woman, and she found herself in a kitchen. Of course, that door was the back entrance. She should have thought of that.

The woman was pouring a glass of milk when the little bell rang, from a couple of rooms away. "That blasted bell!" snorted the woman. "I'd like to take it and break it over her noble Pruitt head!"

"Judith! Judith Cooper!" came Mrs. Pruitt's excited voice.

"I'll be right back," said Judith Cooper grimly, and charged off in the direction of the commotion.

Obviously this was a good time to sneak away. But Erikka was hooked now. She wanted to see what all the noise was about. Had anything terrible happened?

She stood on her toes and leaned out the kitchen door. All she could see was some sort of pantry, with shining crystal and stacks of gold-rimmed dishes.

Judith Cooper suddenly came barreling through the swinging door. "Get on back to the kitchen, you," she said, not unkindly. She pulled down small fragile glasses from a shelf and a bottle of some dark liquid and put them on a silver tray. "They're at the sherry stage," said Judith cheerfully. "Happens every night like clockwork."

When she had whizzed away (and she moved remarkably fast for a woman her size), Erikka sat down on a chair in the kitchen and suddenly smiled. Of course, here she was, in a terrible situation; she could be caught any second and ruin the whole maneuver, but somehow it seemed funny. Judith Cooper was *nice*. Erikka had remembered her as a fierce woman. But she wasn't.

"Does your aunt know you're here?" asked Judith when she came back.

"No. And don't tell her. I'm supposed to meet her outside," said Erikka. "It would ruin everything if she knew I was here. And if the Pruitts knew."

"I've seen you before, very recently," said Judith, scrutinizing Erikka. "Here?"

"Yes," admitted Erikka. "I came with a friend of mine a few nights ago—last week sometime. I'm here for a different reason tonight."

"Sounds sneaky and underhanded," said Judith Cooper, "and I love sneakiness. What's up?"

Erikka didn't know what to say.

"Look, you've got nothing to fear from me," said Judith, nodding her small head vigorously. "I'm quitting the Pruitts' service. I've had enough. Enough. I'm going to leave them in the lurch, so to speak. Without so much as a by-your-leave, as they say. Without so much as a good-bye note. So you don't have to worry about me. And believe me, nothing you could tell me about the Pruitts would surprise me. I could tell *you* some tales, if I chose."

Erikka didn't know why she believed her. But she did. She really believed that Judith Cooper was telling the truth about her feelings toward the Pruitts. Maybe it was because Erikka had seen how the Pruitts treated her. *Anyone* would rebel. It was perfectly understandable.

So Erikka told her about Walt Whitman and the precious volume of poetry that she was sure the Pruitts had stolen from Mr. Tolyukov. Judith continued in her dinner preparations, listening intently, nodding and clucking and saying things like: "The villains! The rogues! The scoundrels!" so often that Erikka began to be afraid Judith would rush into the living room and start beating them up.

"I couldn't say whether or not they have that book," Judith admitted. "They have a lot of books. And they keep them all over the place."

She opened up the crisper and took out things to make a salad; from the pantry she brought several avocados.

"Oh, my favorite." Erikka reached to touch the skin that felt like freshly waxed linoleum, and held one to her face to put the cold on her cheek.

"Alligator pears, they used to call them, back in the Days of Yore," said Judith. "Don't think much of them. But if you like them, take them. *They'll* never miss a thing."

"I couldn't! That's stealing," said Erikka.

"Call it a gift. I do the shopping around here," said Judith. "Besides, I get a certain amount of household money to buy my own meals and I never spend it. I try to watch my waistline." She rolled her eyes to the ceiling. "You'll find a paper bag in the drawer under the breadboard. Might as well stock up. I have a feeling that your auntie is going to be in with those two for quite a while.

You want a cookie or something?"

"No, thanks," said Erikka politely.

"Take a cookie," ordered Judith. Erikka obliged.

"What are they doing in there?" Erikka asked, after some munching.

"Looking at books. Mrs. Hexler Pruitt is doing all the talking, as usual. Mr. Pruitt is looking bilious. Your auntie seems to be just sitting and oohing and aahing a lot. Must be bored to tears."

Just then the phone rang.

"Hexler Pruitt residence, Judith Cooper speaking," said the maid, deftly slicing some celery while she listened.

"Oh, how are you, Mrs. Frinkle . . . Yes, I will . . . Fine, goodbye."

"Was that Dolly Frinkle?" asked Erikka faintly.

"The same. She's on her way down. She lives on the twenty-first floor. She's coming for dinner, I think. A screwball."

"Uh . . ."

"What is it?"

Erikka couldn't speak.

"Out with it, child," said Judith Cooper.

Erikka murmured a few low words about Dolly Frinkle and Aunt Kristina and imminent doom.

Judith grasped the situation at once. "You mean, if Dolly Frinkle comes and says, 'But I never saw this woman before in my life,' everything will be exposed and ruined?"

"Exactly," moaned Erikka.

"Leave it to me. Stay right here. Don't worry about the Pruitts coming in here; they wouldn't know a kitchen if they were run over by one." Judith whipped from the table and out the swinging doors.

A minute later she was back, carrying the paper bag with the avocados in it. "Now look, I just told your auntie that she received an urgent call to return home at once. She looked rather startled, but got up to get her coat. The Pruitts are seeing her to the door. Come on. We can stand in the kitchen and hear their goodbyes." She pulled Erikka across the floor to the door.

"Whitman was of tremendous importance," Mrs. Pruitt was saying. "I just adore his work. I love everything about it. It's so—so musical!"

"Regina loves music," growled Browler Pruitt helpfully.

" 'I hear America singing, the varied carols I hear!' " said Regina. "Oh, isn't it wonderful, Miss Angstrand? 'The delicious singing of the mother—or of the young wife at work—or of the girl sewing or washing . . .' It is all so thoroughly *American*. Can you imagine a Russian owning this book? It was a disgrace. A cultural outrage. We were overjoyed to be able to acquire this volume from him."

"No doubt," said Aunt Kristina. "But I really must go. I am afraid there has been some emergency."

"If you would leave us your phone number, we could contact you for dinner sometime," said Regina. "It's too bad you couldn't stay tonight."

"Perhaps I'll call you," said Aunt Kristina. Then Erikka heard the elevator doors open.

"Charming woman. A real artist," said Regina Hexler Pruitt to her husband. "Not like the frauds we run into most of the time."

The hall was empty. "You can take the next elevator and catch up with your auntie in the lobby," said Judith Cooper. "Look: good luck, Erikka. If your old Russian friend ever needs a party catered, look me up. I'm starting my own business."

" 'Bye. And thanks," whispered Erikka.

"Here. Don't forget your avocados." Judith thrust the bag at her. Erikka grabbed them and ran.

She caught up with Aunt Kristina in the front of the apartment building. Her aunt was looking wildly about for her.

"Did you call the Pruitts?" she asked fearfully as Erikka came running up to her.

"No," said Erikka. "There was no call. But I was there. I was in the kitchen talking to the maid. And I told her a little about what was going on—"

"You're crazy!"

"It's okay. Dolly Frinkle had called and was about to come over. So I had to get you out of there before she showed up. The maid is nice. She gave me some avocados."

"Let's move quickly," said Aunt Kristina. "If that maid should let on what was happening—"

"She won't," said Erikka confidently, and then she didn't talk at all, almost running to keep up with her aunt.

The full moon was higher and the sky was darker as they took the homebound el. Aunt Kristina began to smile a bit. "I suppose there was no harm done," she said. "Maybe Dolly Frinkle will just think that she forgot meeting me. And there was no sneakiness on our part, so there'll be no reason for them to be suspicious."

"You *did* see the book, then."

"I did, Erikka. And if that belonged to your Mr. Tolyukov, he was a lucky man—up until it was stolen. It is a beautiful volume. The Pruitts talked about other things first, about music and the ballet and the museums they donate to, and then they got around to their rare books. And your friend the violinist was right. They went and got that book from some other room. Mrs. Pruitt was as eager as you can imagine that I see their prize possession. She kept talking about how much they had gone through to get that book. I just smiled and admired it, and they were both as proud of it as if they had given birth to it themselves."

"How much they had gone through!" cried Erikka. "They had gone through Mr. Tolyukov's boxes and chest and treasures and whole apartment. The creeps. Now when we get home I'm going to call the police."

"As you wish," said Aunt Kristina. "Are you going to tell them how you know that they have it?"

"I don't know. I'll think about that for a while."

The train sped along. Erikka stared at the streets and buildings and mounds of dirty snow. Tomorrow was May. Tomorrow was moving day. And maybe things would work out all right after all.

"I have to say that both of the Pruitts seem very much interested in literature and art," said Aunt Kristina. "It seems to be a serious and a sincere interest, too, even if it's manifested in a criminal manner."

"I don't believe it," said Erikka. "How could they? They're common crooks."

"Erikka, the most common crook in the world can love poetry," said Aunt Kristina soothingly. "The wonderful things in the world are not reserved only for the solid upright citizens. Anyone can love Mozart. Anyone can love the paintings of Chagall. Saint and sinner alike can sit and smile and tap their feet when a waltz is played."

Erikka turned and stared out the window again. Could it be that terrible Regina Hexler Pruitt could love water-color paintings as much as she, Erikka, did? Could it be that old stuffy Pruitt enjoyed violin music as much as Francisco did? Or that the two of them, scoundrels and liars both, loved the poetry of Walt Whitman as much as Tolyukov? She didn't know if it was possible.

But if it were, wouldn't the opposite be true, too? That maybe genuinely good people might be oblivious to the beauties of art and music?

All she could think of, as the train went speeding toward Merriam Street, was that Tolyukov deserved the book he treasured so much.

Suddenly she felt chilly. There was so much left to do: call the police, tell them what she knew, go see Tolyukov tomorrow for the last time, when he moved across town . . .

She stood to button her coat and handed the paper bag to Aunt Kristina to hold.

"Are you cold? We should have taken a taxi," said Kristina.

Ordinarily Erikka would have been crushed at the thought of having missed a possible taxi ride. Only once had she ridden in one. But now she had other things on her mind. She just shook her head and buttoned her coat up to her neck.

Kristina rose from her seat because their station was coming next. She handed the bag to Erikka. "That's a lot of avocados," she said. "Must be five or six, by the weight of them."

The doors slid open. "No," said Erikka as she hurried out onto the platform, "just a couple."

"That's more than a couple," insisted Kristina.

Erikka stopped under a light and opened the bag. "Look, it's just . . . just . . ." she said, her voice trailing away.

She drew out a second parcel, something wrapped in brown velvet. And she knew what it must be.

Aunt Kristina grabbed it and opened the folds of cloth. There it was: Tolyukov's precious book, just as he had last seen it.

"It's Judith Cooper's doing!" breathed Erikka. "I didn't

do it, Aunt Kristina! Honest. I promised."

"I know you didn't," said Aunt Kristina soberly. "But now you have it."

Erikka didn't know whether to laugh or cry. Oh, sure, it was great to have it, to be able to give it to Tolyukov tomorrow as a going-away present! But that was just the trouble. Now she couldn't call the police and accuse the Pruitts of stealing the book—because they didn't have it any more. They could deny ever having seen it. And now Tolyukov had nothing to bargain with. The Pruitts would come and pay their final bill, and he would still have his book, and he would love it, but it would do him no good.

Aunt Kristina seemed to know what was going on in Erikka's mind. She reached out and stroked Erikka's long hair and didn't say a word.

Then they turned and went down the steps to Merriam Street, and the full moon shone over their shoulders.

Chapter Fifteen

THE COLLAPSE

It was dinnertime when Aunt Kristina and Erikka turned up Merriam Street toward the Knorrs' apartment. Traffic had started to move again after the storm, and speeding cars splashed curtains of water from the gutters. Erikka sneezed several times. "I really ought to have called a cab," said Aunt Kristina, "with you so recently sick."

Erikka didn't answer, she just clutched the paper bag close to her and thought and thought.

"Thank you, Aunt Kristina," she said suddenly, skidding to a stop just before they reached the door to the Knorrs' apartment. "I know you didn't have to do this today. I'm glad you helped me out."

"My pleasure." Aunt Kristina hugged her.

"Back so soon?" Erikka withdrew from her aunt's embrace at the sound of her mother's voice.

"Mission accomplished," said Aunt Kristina gaily.

"Well, you're just in time to help me carry some groceries upstairs," said Mrs. Knorr. "But I have to step in the deli first, to pay the month's bill."

"We'll wait," said Erikka, and the three of them entered the deli.

Erikka sneezed again, as Mrs. Knorr was writing out a check.

"Too much gallivanting," said Mrs. Knorr. "That germ is still making the rounds, Erikka; you ought to be more careful."

"I'm *fine*, Mommy! It's Inga who's sick now, remember?"

Florry took the check. "Just let me write you a receipt, Mrs. K., and then we're all set," she said, her fingers dancing over the keys of the cash register and punching all the right ones. Her bracelets jangled musically.

Erikka leaned against the glass case. She was tired. So much had been accomplished today, but there was a lot left to do. First, she had to have supper. And then, if she could get permission to go out, she had to bring the book to Tolyukov and tell Francisco that his plan had worked, much better than he had intended. *Then,* when she came home, she had to light the old candle and go to see Theresa Maloy.

Tomorrow's the last day for a lot of things, she thought. Old Tolyukov will be gone from the store on Ingoldsby Street. And the candle will by then have burned down to the bottom—there will be no more midnight trips to Canaan Lake.

Aunt Kristina would be flying back to Boston tomorrow night. And then Inga and Annie would finally move back to their own bedroom and Erikka would have her privacy again.

But then she would have to give the candlestick back to Tolyukov. It was only collateral, anyway; he would give her the blue vase that had belonged to her first mother.

And then everything would be back to normal, except there would be a gaping hole in her life where the bookstore had been . . .

"Erikka, don't lean against the glass," said Mrs. Knorr.

"Here's your receipt," said Florry. "Enjoying the snow?"

"Snow," said Mrs. Knorr. She leaned against Erikka.

"All right, don't push," said Erikka. "I'm not leaning hard. Stop it." She straightened up, but her mother continued to slope heavily against her.

"Mrs. K.!" said Florry in a loud voice.

Erikka stood erect, and her mother staggered against the counter and then thudded to the floor.

"Oh, God, she's dead," cried Florry, rushing from behind the counter. Erikka and Aunt Kristina knelt on either side of Mrs. Knorr. Erikka couldn't see clearly through the instantaneous mist of tears. Her mother's face was white, white like snow, like the blank paper Kristina painted on . . . her eyes were rolled back in her head; all that was visible were the bloodshot whites . . .

The customers in the deli had leaped up and crowded around the Knorrs. Erikka wanted to turn and spring at them in rage. But a young woman poked her way through the crowd and knelt down beside the insensible Mrs. Knorr. "I'm a nurse," she said calmly, and Aunt Kristina and Erikka and Florry moved back so she could get through. Deftly she loosened Mrs. Knorr's scarf and undid the top button of her blouse. "Do you have some ammonia?" she asked Florry, "and a blanket?"

Florry scrambled to her feet. "Okay, folks, the evening performance is over," she called over her shoulder as she went searching for some ammonia. "Get back, please."

The customers retreated about six inches.

The young woman was checking pulse and respiration. "I think it's just a faint," she said. "Has this woman been sick lately, does anyone know?"

"No!" said Erikka.

"There's been a bout of something, some virus in the family," said Aunt Kristina.

"Hmmmm," said the young woman, and took the ammonia that Florry thrust at her. She quickly splashed a little on her handkerchief and held it up to Mrs. Knorr's nose.

Erikka watched as her mother began to resist the strong odor and to feebly try to push the handkerchief away.

"Might she be pregnant?" asked the nurse.

"I don't know," said Kristina. "Should we call an ambulance?"

"I don't think so. Let's wait and see," said the nurse.

Mrs. Knorr began to shake her head and open her eyes. Aunt Kristina leaned forward quickly. "Sharon, it's me.

Are you all right? Does anything hurt? How do you feel?"

"It's okay," said Mrs. Knorr weakly. "Let me rest a bit. It's just a fainting spell." She closed her eyes for a minute and then opened them again. "Where's Erikka?" she asked.

"Right here, Mommy," said Erikka, crouching up close to her mother and reaching out her hand.

"Why don't you go upstairs and mind the kids till I come up? I left them with Inga, but she's still out of sorts. And don't mention this to them, it'd only scare them." Mrs. Knorr closed her eyes again.

Erikka didn't move.

"I think you can go," said the nurse kindly. "There's nothing to worry about."

Erikka shook her head.

After a while, Mrs. Knorr seemed a little better. She sat down on a chair for about ten minutes to regain her strength. When she saw that Erikka hadn't gone upstairs, she didn't say anything about it. The nurse tried to pay for her roast beef on rye, but Florry wouldn't hear of it. "A regular Florence Nightingale, that one," she said tearfully after the nurse had left. "The likes of which this humble deli shall not see again. Not every day, at least. Noble character."

"I feel better now," said Mrs. Knorr, standing, but leaning on Aunt Kristina for support. "Let's go upstairs."

Erikka managed all the groceries, as Aunt Kristina

helped her mother up the narrow front steps.

Annie and Bengt were quietly watching television in the front room when they came in. Mrs. Knorr went straight to her bedroom and shut the door.

Erikka and Aunt Kristina got the supper. Aunt Kristina said that she was sure that it was the flu. After all, it had gone around from Erikka to Annie to Inga; it was natural that Mrs. Knorr should catch it.

"Just the same," said Kristina, "I'm glad we happened to be there when she fainted."

After supper Erikka wanted to run down to the bookstore and give Tolyukov his book. But Aunt Kristina said no. She said that Erikka had been sneezing and sniffling all afternoon ("I wasn't sniffling, I was out and out crying," said Erikka pointedly) and that, in the absence of her mother, Erikka was going to have to obey her aunt. "You can go down first thing in the morning," she said consolingly.

"At least I can call him on the phone, can't I?" asked Erikka sullenly.

"Of course."

But all Erikka got was a recording. *The number you have dialed is out of order or temporarily disconnected. Please consult your directory or your local operator. This is a recording.* Of course: his phone had been disconnected because he was moving.

Aunt Kristina came out of Mrs. Knorr's bedroom and said, "She feels fine now, Erikka, just a little weak. She says to thank you for not mentioning this to the others. She's going to stay in bed till morning."

Erikka went into her bedroom and closed the door, as far as she could, considering Toby was still blocking it. She was angry at her aunt for not allowing her to go see Tolyukov. She was a little angry at Judith Cooper for secreting the book in the bag of avocados. And she was worried about her mother, immensely worried.

She leaned back on her bed and looked up at the water-color and the candlestick. There they stood on her dresser, like decorations on some altar. The watercolor with its glowing images, and the heavy golden candlestick, with its candle all but burned out completely, with the tears of wax rolling down and getting caught in the fancy knobs and scrolls of the metalwork.

One without the other would not work, she thought dreamily. If I had had just the painting, it would have been just a painting, even though it was beautiful. And the same with the candle. Just a fancy antique candlestick from some church in Russia. What was the magic ingredient? Just that they stood together in the same place?

Two lights, thought Erikka. The glow of the candle-light and the glow of the full moon—for it was full, the moon; it had grown in the picture during the past two weeks; it had been a crescent slipper at first, but now it was like a mammoth pearl in the sky.

She closed her eyes and threw her arms over her face, thinking about what she would say when she saw Theresa tonight . . .

Chapter Sixteen

FULL MOON, FLICKERING CANDLE

Her dream was rife with impossible pairings. Under an electric-blue night sky, with a cream-colored full moon like an opalescent fruit swimming overhead, a cast of extraordinary characters met and talked, nodded and clucked. Doreen O'Donald and old Tolyukov. Aunt Kristina and Dolly Frinkle and Mr. Knorr. The Countess Olga Molokiev (in her skirt and blouse, smiling) and the Countess Olga Molokiev (in her whiskers and fur, purring). Simon Cameron and Florry and Inga. Francisco de Medina and Martha Wong and Browler Pruitt. Her first mother with Bengt on her lap. Theresa Maloy and Annie and Regina Hexler Pruitt. And they were all murmuring things Erikka couldn't hear; they were all sharing worry for Erikka's second mother, who was off to the side, on a slab of stone, eyes closed. Erikka wanted to circle all these sympathetic people, reach the stone, and wake her second mother up. But over there was out of bounds and she couldn't go.

The big ripe moon was setting.

She clutched at her covers in the dark and blinked her

eyes. She could hear the regular breathing of her two sisters, and beyond that the chunking and gear shifting of early-morning delivery trucks on Merriam Street. The moon would be down by now. She had slept clear through till almost dawn. She nearly screamed.

One hand on the bedstead, she groped for the alarm clock and held it close. Six-thirty. She hadn't ever tried to cross through the picture during the day—it had seemed that the moon was an essential key in the traveling. But she had no other choice. She felt impelled by the crazy dream to seek out Theresa immediately—and she didn't know why.

The sulfur from the struck match stung her nostrils. When the flame was steady, she dropped the matches on the dresser and lifted the candlestick and, like a boat on a misty river, moved slowly and surely through the chilling thickness.

It was a different mountainside that Erikka stepped into this last time. The deep shadows were gone, the ink of darkest night was gone. The trees stood solemn in the grayness; the closer ones took on a super-real clarity, almost a photographic exactness, but the farther trees were indistinct in the mist.

Gray fog, gray light, gray mountain mist. The night was leaving and these were the first grays of the morning. There was no sun, not yet, but the vapors from the forest floor were rising and the woods were shrouded.

She guarded the flame with her left hand, supported the candlestick with her right, and pushed her way to the path.

At the door to Theresa Maloy's cabin, Erikka paused for a minute. Should she knock? She didn't want to scare her. And it was so early in the morning—so late in the night—certainly Theresa wouldn't be expecting her now. But as she stood, uncertain, a drop of hot wax rolled off the candle onto her thumb. No time to stand thinking about it. So she opened the door.

"Theresa?" She raised the candle up so she could see in the gloomy room.

Theresa was there, under several shawls, lying on the bed and rubbing her eyes.

"Who?" Her voice was forceful but rough from disuse.

"It's me." Erikka set the candle down on the center table and hurried to Theresa's bedside. "I'm so sorry I'm so late —I woke you up—but look, the candle's burned down so far, and I wanted to come one more time to see you."

"Oh, daughter." Theresa felt her own forehead. "Such a fever! Such a tiredness. Like all of old age, landing ka-lump on my bones all at once for the first time. Such a heaviness. Here, pull me up."

"You don't feel well?"

"Umphh." Theresa, sitting up, shook her head, and her hair was like a gray rag falling off her scalp. She scooped it into a rope and a loop and fixed it with a hair-pin. "There. More beautiful for my company, who comes to see me uninvited at the oddest hours." She smiled. "To my great delight. Yes, I am sick, am laid out on this bed like a corpse, with all the sneezings and fevers and accompanying ills. But I feel better now; even to see you my body adjusts itself."

"I brought you that cold," said Erikka. "I did. I'm a walking ambassador of disease. I've given it to everyone. I'm so sorry."

"Eh, no harm done. You get over these things. You right yourself, or your good body rights itself and you be healthy again. It's the way of things."

Erikka reached out and took Theresa's thin wrist in her hand. "I came tonight to see you," she said, and as she spoke she realized the words had been piling up at the back of her throat for a long time. "I didn't come to see the hills or the moon or the trees or my private new world. I came to see you, just one last time, because I wanted to, because I like you. I won't be able to come again. The candle is sputtering already."

"No need to sneer at the moon and trees," said Theresa, looking pleased. "But I'm happy for your coming, daughter. You are not without a heart. You feel something even for old cranky Theresa. This is a thing which makes me glad."

Erikka felt joy.

"And your candle sinks, and the time for our visit is closing. The door is closing, crash," said Theresa. She pulled herself to her feet and went awkwardly around the room. "Presents for the parting. Presents for my daughter. Where is the—oh, here." From the chest in the shadows she drew a sack, a cloth sack. "For your esteemed parents. For your precious brothers and sisters." She threw things in the sack. "For you, some more beads and rings and woman's things."

"Stop. I don't need presents," cried Erikka. "You've given me your mother's necklace, which I'm saving for some very special time." She stayed Theresa's twiggy hands in her warm ones. She took the necklaces, heavy old things stiff with intricate metalwork and jewels, and arranged them on Theresa's neck. "These are yours. I don't need them," Erikka said.

"Of course you don't need them. But I give them, here, take—"

"No, you keep them. They are your treasures," said Erikka. "I have my own already."

Theresa fingered the old strands around her neck, and looked at Erikka quizzically, and smiled.

When they stepped outside, they were caught in a spill of early-morning light. The mists were still there, hovering in the branches of trees, dulling the sounds of wind and bird. But they were not gray mists; they shone bronze, light through a jar of honey. The world had lost its sharpness and nearness. There were only faint suggestions that this wasn't all a dream, only occasional reminders, like the roughness of the path underfoot and the pungent, nose-wrinkling smell of the pines. Erikka and Theresa passed through the amber woods. From only a few feet away, they would have looked like a golden nightgown and a golden shawl-and-skirt, carrying a sack lumpy with golden bulges.

"The full moon is gone," said Erikka, when they had reached the clearing. "And the candle is almost burned out. Look, there's just a little heap of wax and wick left. It's time to say goodbye."

"Oh, daughter," said Theresa. "Goodness and badness are in the parting of friends. I miss you."

"You should come to Chicago," said Erikka.

"Maybe someday," said Theresa. "I have your address in my pocket."

"Please," Erikka set the candlestick down and looked at the old woman.

"Oh, we must say goodbye," said Theresa Maloy. She reached out her arms, her shawl like webbing around them, and folded Erikka in. "Goodbye, daughter."

"Goodbye." Erikka felt a salty wetness in her eyes and in the back of her nose and mouth. She squeezed her eyes closed tight and ducked her head against Theresa's shoulder, out of view, out of the wind that had just sprung up with the warming day.

The wind.

Springing up, whistling suddenly about in the mists and trees, turning, twisting Erikka's hair about her face, rippling Theresa's shawl, ripping the mists apart for a minute to let the full sun through, and then wrenching the flame from the candle. A thread of charcoal-colored smoke was all that remained.

And, before their eyes, before their horrified eyes, the whole candlestick disappeared.

Chapter Seventeen

THE WAY HOME

The wind rose, and Erikka was distressed.

"Now, daughter," said Theresa feebly, stretching out her hand, but there was nothing to suggest, and her hand fell back against her skirt.

"I can't stay here." Erikka's words were thickened by tears. Her mother was sick, lying in bed, and Aunt Kristina would come in the bedroom to wake the girls up and Erikka would be gone, and how could Kristina know that Erikka was stuck in her painting, standing in a clearing in the mountains of upstate New York? And Annie would cry, and Inga would cry, and they would think she had been kidnapped, and Bengt would cry because the others were crying—and her mother, her mother would wonder if she had run away!

"I have to go back," said Erikka stubbornly.

"Now, daughter," Theresa said, "don't worry. We go to Albany and I send you home on a plane. You are home by tomorrow."

A whole day! A whole day away from home, with them

worrying and blaming themselves. With her mother sick and frightened.

"Erikka, come. We go down to the road," said Theresa. "We catch a ride to Elizabethtown and see if there's a bus or something to Albany."

Erikka couldn't move. Her tears just streamed. How could she go on a bus and a plane in her nightgown with the red roses on it? She was like a tree: rooted, immobile, leaning in the winds of this catastrophe. So she just stood there, head bowed, eyes brimming.

And then Theresa grabbed Erikka's wrist, as tightly as a pair of pliers on a stubborn rusty bolt. She said something strange, something garbled and guttural, and stared and pointed.

She *is* a witch, thought Erikka wildly; after all this time, she's uttering incantations and spells, words I can't understand in some weird language!

And there, hovering in mid-air, like a dragonfly with racing wings, was a small piece of light. A rosebud of light, a spearhead of light, small but distinct, white in the copper mist.

"God save us!" Erikka whispered.

Underneath the light a form appeared, a long form, chunky and quickly thickening. Attached to it by a looping trail was another form, settling on the ground, moving forward, flushing from ghostly suggestion to pure, real flesh . . .

"I *told* you," said a triumphant voice.

"I don't believe it," said a second voice, and then they were there, two-thirds of the Three Terrors, Annie and Inga, holding hands. And Annie held the candlestick.

Erikka rushed up to Annie and kissed her. "Yuck," said Annie.

"Hey, this is neat, Erikka," said Inga, looking around. "Where are we?"

"Here and almost gone," cried Erikka in joy. The candlestick had just a fingernail's worth of wax left to burn. "Quick, Inga, let's go. Theresa, goodbye!" Erikka grabbed the sack and hooked her free hand around Annie's waist. "Turn around, Annie, and walk into the shadows, and blow the candle out, quick."

Theresa was stumbling forward, suddenly crying herself, her hand raised to bless Erikka one last time. The wind swelled and was full-bodied on the shapes of the pine boughs and the girls holding hands; Erikka had turned to call "Goodbye!" to Theresa, and maybe she got it out and maybe she didn't. Through the thickness they fell, arms and cloth sack and hair streaming and the wind around them, energy, benevolence; and then they were back.

In Erikka Knorr's bedroom: Inga, and Annie with the candle that was now completely burned out, and Erikka with eyes still wet and a heart still thudding inside her, and Theresa, who was just regaining her balance.

Chapter Eighteen

AFLOAT
ON THE SEAS
OF GOD

Theresa sat on Erikka's bed to get her breath back and closed her eyes. Inga and Erikka stood staring at one another in relief. Annie climbed on Toby, glancing shyly at Theresa every once in a while.

"What *happened?*" Inga was saying desperately.

"No, you tell me," said Erikka, setting down the candlestick with a thump.

Inga perched on the edge of Annie's cot. "Annie and I woke up and found you gone. And while we were sitting here wondering, all of a sudden the candlestick appeared on the dresser. There was no flame, just a puff of smoke, like someone had just blown it out. *I* was petrified, but Annie was perfectly calm. She said, 'Come on, Inga, us too,' and got up and found your matches on the dresser and then she said, 'I've watched Erikka do this lots,' and then she started to—to walk into the picture. I grabbed her hand to hold her back but I got pulled in instead. Who's *she?*" Inga nodded at Theresa.

"An old friend."

"Well, I can see she's old," said Inga under her breath. "She looks like a witch."

Elephant-ears Annie heard this. She scrambled down off Toby and went to Erikka's bed. "Are you a witch?" said Annie loudly.

Theresa opened her eyes. She started to laugh. "I might be crazy, but I'm not a witch," she said.

"Did anyone know I was gone?" Erikka asked Inga.

"No."

"Thank God. Now, Inga, you can't say anything about this—"

"Really." Inga was insulted. "I know when to keep my mouth shut. Don't you think you'd better threaten our little Martha Wong?"

But just then Aunt Kristina came to the door. Her mouth dropped open at the sight of the old woman sitting on Erikka's bed.

"Who's this?"

Erikka couldn't speak. Inga stood still. Theresa smiled charmingly, and Annie said, "It's a friend."

"Erikka, your mother wants to see you," said Kristina. "Um—would you care for a cup of tea, ma'am?"

"Nothing I'd like better," said Theresa, sliding her feet to the floor. "Traveling tends to be wearying."

Erikka opened the door to her mother's room.

Mrs. Knorr was sitting up in bed, waiting. She was wearing an old flannel shirt against the cold, and a thick book from the library was opened next to her.

"Are you feeling better?" asked Erikka.

"Much better," said Mrs. Knorr. "I'll be up in a few minutes. But I wanted to talk to you alone first."

"You have the flu, you shouldn't get up," said Erikka.

"I don't have the flu."

"You have the faints, then."

"Not the faints, either. I'm fine. I'll be up and putting together a nice festive lunch for Aunt Kristina—she'll be leaving on an evening flight tonight. I want to have a little buffet. I thought maybe you could call the florist on the corner and have him send up some flowers. Some yellow roses. To show her how nice it's been to have her here."

Erikka couldn't help it. "But yellow roses are so lovely and extravagant," she said bluntly.

"So they are," said Mrs. Knorr. "But Kristina likes them. So for once we'll splurge."

"Should you be getting up so soon after being sick?"

"I'm as healthy as a horse," said Mrs. Knorr. "I guess it's time to tell you, however. There's going to be a new baby in this family."

"A what?" said Erikka.

Mrs. Knorr laughed. "Now don't get hysterical. A baby."

"But—your classes—a baby? A real live one?" Erikka sounded silly, even to herself. She knelt on the edge of her mother's bed and bounced. "Will it be all ours? Can it sleep in my room?"

"I'll take a leave of absence, work on my dissertation at home. We'll see. Let's wait till it comes before we decide where it'll sleep."

"Well, *congratulations*," said Erikka. She flopped herself up to the head of the bed and kissed her mother solemnly. And then she and her mother both began to laugh.

After Theresa had had her tea, and Mrs. Knorr had called Inga and Annie and Bengt into her room to tell them about the new baby, and after they had all decided on their favorite names for a boy and a girl baby, or two boys and two girls, in case it was twins, they sat down to breakfast. It was Aunt Kristina who said, "Erikka, aren't you going to the bookstore this morning?"

Erikka dropped the orange she had been peeling and looked at the clock. It was nine-thirty.

"The Pruitts might have come and gone by now," she said. "And I want them to see that their sneaky schemes have been thwarted. I want them to see me give Tolyukov his book back, so they know I took it and not him. I've got to go, right now."

"Well, hurry," said Aunt Kristina. "Call up the old man and tell him to stall the Pruitts until you get there."

"His line's been disconnected because he's moving," called Erikka as she tore down the hall to get her jacket.

"Well, call Francisco; didn't you say he lives next door?" said Aunt Kristina. "May I come with you?"

Erikka ran back in the kitchen and started thumbing

through the telephone book. "Sure. Let's see—de Marco, de Mayo, Dembrowski, Demby—de Medina, F." She dialed the number. Everyone in the kitchen held their breath.

"Francisco? Oh, thank God. Look—have you seen the Pruitts go into the store yet?—can you see if you lean out your window? They're two middle-aged people, dressed for the slaughter—they're *there?* Oh, Francisco, do something! We've got the book! Stall them! I want them to know that it's back where it belongs!—it's better than nothing."

There was a silence. Erikka twined the telephone cord around her arm.

"The *book,* Francisco! The Whitman! We have it!"

More silence.

"Exactly. Do something. Lock the door on them, or go in and pretend to hold the store up—anything. Just keep them there for fifteen minutes! I'm leaving right now."

Suddenly Aunt Kristina took the phone out of Erikka's hand. "Francisco, play your violin. They can't resist good music." And then she hung up.

Erikka's face fell. The Pruitts wouldn't delay their business for good music. Not such miserable, wicked people as they . . .

"Come on," said Erikka, swallowing her disappointment. "Maybe we can make it." Aunt Kristina grabbed her coat.

"I'm coming, too," said Inga, pushing herself away from the table.

"Me, too," said Annie.

"Me, too," said Theresa. They all looked at her.

"Well, I don't want to be left alone here," she said.

"I'll call a taxi," said Aunt Kristina decisively. "It'll come in five minutes, but it'll get us there in a flash."

"Where are we going?" asked Theresa. Bengt was the only one not struggling to get into a jacket. Bengt just smiled.

"Hey, where are you all going?" called Mrs. Knorr from her room, hearing the running footsteps and Erikka's screaming instructions.

"To restore a book to its rightful owner!" called Erikka as she flew past her mother's door. "This time it's a crisis of epic proportions for sure!"

"On an adventure," yelled Inga. "We'll be back in time for lunch."

"Just out for a half hour, Sharon," said Aunt Kristina, pausing breathlessly in the doorway. "I'll pick up a few things for lunch."

"No need, Florry's going to do a little marketing for me," said Mrs. Knorr. "Where are you going?"

"We're going to San Francisco," said Annie. "To get a baby."

"Where *are* we going?" came the voice of an old woman, someone whom Mrs. Knorr didn't recognize.

And then the apartment was silent.

The taxi came quickly, screeching to a stop, pushing a bubbly sheet of puddle onto their clothes. Bengt and

Annie screamed in delight. Aunt Kristina shoved them all into the cab. "Ingoldsby Street. The bookstore, the old one," said Aunt Kristina, falling into the front seat.

"On the double!" said Inga.

The cab driver was an honorable man. He sped away down Merriam Street, squealing his tires and roaring his engine. "Matter of life and death?" He grinned, spinning the steering wheel with one hand.

"At least," said Inga.

"Where are we going?" asked Theresa patiently, trying to disengage the edge of her shawl, which had gotten caught in the door.

"Ingoldsby Street bookstore," said the cab driver.

The sun spun gold in the sky. It was May Day, Erikka suddenly remembered, so she rolled down the window and let the wind rush in. All their hair flew around.

The book, in its folds of brown velvet, lay in her lap.

The cab let them out at the corner. Erikka and the Three Terrors ran on ahead, while Aunt Kristina pawed through her purse for change and Theresa worked at freeing her shawl without ripping it.

"Shhh," said Erikka.

The four children ran on tiptoe down the side alley, splashing in puddles and dodging crates. Bengt wanted to stop and play in a puddle, but Annie yanked him along.

The back door was open.

Into the empty room they stole, the four Knorr children. Erikka had to stifle a moan, to see all of Tolyukov's things cleared out. Without them, this comfortable room was nothing, just a room, four walls and a ceiling and floor.

There was something else, though. It was the sound of a violin. Erikka stood still, her spine tingling, her skin thrilling to the sound. Inga stood still. Even Annie and Bengt, holding hands, listened.

Francisco was playing, was dealing out music in the front room, pouring it out like water from a spring. The notes splashed forth and rolled around the rooms, immaterial as light, ineffably direct. A salute, a command, and it was impossible to ignore. The music was a miracle.

And Erikka stood, suddenly sure of herself, anointed by the brilliant sound.

The music swelled, flushed, telescoped, and then wound to a close on one long somber note.

"Chaconne in D minor, by Johann Sebastian Bach," Francisco was saying quietly.

"But it's marvelous. You're a gifted soul," cried the enthusiastic voice of Regina Hexler Pruitt. "You've the technique, the interpretation, the inspiration—how wonderful that you happened to stop by! What a treat for us all."

Erikka went to the door. The front room was stripped of everything but vacant bookshelves and a few people. The Pruitts were standing by the door, patting Francisco on the back. Old Tolyukov, with the Countess Olga Molokiev in his arms, was leaning on the empty counter stroking her. And Simon Cameron was sitting on the window ledge looking glum.

"Mr. Tolyukov?" said Erikka softly.

He looked up and smiled wanly. Erikka went to him and put the parcel in front of him.

"The book?" he asked, his eyebrows arching in surprise. Erikka nodded.

"Thank you," he said.

Mrs. Pruitt and Mr. Pruitt were buttoning their coats. "Now all accounts are settled, payments made and books cleared, yes?" said Browler Pruitt.

"Yes," said Tolyukov. "I'm all through with the book business, as you see. Ready to move out, even. All that's left here are my cat and my book."

Mrs. Pruitt paused.

"Your book?" she said faintly.

"My Walt Whitman," said Tolyukov.

She took a couple of steps toward him. "But—didn't you—" she began. She turned white.

"You remember this?" said Tolyukov. "It's been missing. But I guess Erikka found it."

"Erikka?" said Pruitt. "Oh, Browler, it can't be."

Browler Pruitt came to her side. Together they looked at the book, which sat on the old linoleum-topped counter.

"It is," said Browler. "Harumph."

"I am beginning to suspect thievery," said Regina Pruitt.

"A little sweet skulduggery?" said Erikka innocently.

Tolyukov wasn't listening. He held the book. "I feel steadfast again," he said, "like the courageous narrator in *Passage to India*. It's not in this edition but it's close to my heart nevertheless." He recited from memory, with his book held to his chest.

> *"Sail forth! steer for the deep waters only!*
> *Reckless, O soul, exploring, I with thee, and thou*
> *   with me;*
> *For we are bound where mariner has not yet dared*
> *   to go,*
> *And we will risk the ship, ourselves and all.*
> *O my brave soul!*
> *O farther, farther sail!*
> *O daring joy, but safe! Are they not all the seas of*
> *   God?*
> *O farther, farther, farther sail!"*

No one stirred. "It's time to go," said Tolyukov.

"The seas of God," murmured Mrs. Pruitt, forgetting her accusations for a moment. "We're all afloat on the seas of God."

Aunt Kristina and Theresa Maloy walked into the bookstore.

Tolyukov closed the book and wrapped it up again in its cloth. Regina Hexler Pruitt put her arm in Browler's— why, she looked sad! Erikka was amazed. Tolyukov handed the blue vase to Erikka. Then everything was quiet for a minute, as Francisco put away his bow and violin and Tolyukov picked up his book and the black cat. "Ready, Countess?" he said, in a funny small voice.

And then Theresa said something in that strange witch language. Erikka stared at her. Was she putting a spell on someone? She was! On old Tolyukov. He was slowly putting down the Countess and the book and looking at Theresa. He was saying something to her—he was talking in the witch language, too.

And then, as the Knorr children and the Pruitts and Simon and Francisco and Aunt Kristina watched, old Modest Mikhailovich Tolyukov said: "Olga," as calmly as if he were saying what kind of soup he'd have for lunch, and he walked over and put his arms around Theresa Maloy.

And Theresa burst into tears.

Chapter Nineteen

ERIKKA'S TURN

Somehow, they all squeezed into the taxi (which Aunt Kristina had thoughtfully asked to wait), Tolyukov and Theresa in the front seat, and Aunt Kristina and Francisco de Medina and Simon Cameron and Erikka and the Three Terrors in the back. "My license will be revoked for sure, if they catch me," said the driver, but he sensed the excitement of the situation and took them anyway. It was only a few blocks.

Mrs. Knorr was arranging the roses in a peanut-butter jar when she heard the downstairs door open and a flood of laughing voices come in. She hurried to the top door.

"We're back, Mommy," shouted Annie, leading the way. And in came a troop of people, some of whom she had never seen before. An old man and an old woman, and a black cat, and a young Filipino carrying a violin case, and that Simon somebody, hanging to the edge of the group but grinning like crazy, and Aunt Kristina looking dazed and carrying Bengt, and Erikka and Inga coming up last. "What is this?" she asked, and was greeted with eight answers all at once.

"It's the Countess! It's the Countess Olga!" said Erikka, louder than the rest. "She's not Theresa Maloy at all. She's Olga Theresa Molokiev!"

"We rided in a taxi, Mommy, but we didn't see no babies," said Annie, galloping in circles around her mother. Bengt joined her.

"Friends of Erikka's. He's just liquidated his bookstore. Isn't it wonderful?" said Aunt Kristina.

"Can you make your violin sound like a trumpet?" Inga was asking Francisco.

"Hold it. Hold it!" cried Mrs. Knorr. "Tell me what's going on!"

So they sat down and told her. Not the part about going into the picture, naturally—nobody mentioned that, not even Annie. They said that Theresa—only now she wanted to be called by her real name, Olga—was a friend of Erikka's and had come a long way to see her. And she had gone to the bookstore and recognized her old fiancé, after a sixty-year absence, and had spoken to him in their mother tongue.

"And I thought it was witch talk," said Erikka. "It was Russian."

"We are lost, we are separated in the course of time and change," said the Countess Olga. "I try and try to find out where Modest is gone away to. And sometimes I think that I have a clue, and I spend years following it up, and it is always to no avail. Then I start to be afraid that I am going crazy. So when I see the candlestick that Erikka holds—well, I don't believe my eyes. I think it is my age and my fond memories playing me tricks. And I am so old. I just don't let myself think that this really is the same candlestick that we get in the Church of St. Nicholas. I don't let myself think about it. Nobody likes to think that they're crazy."

"We were separated. On two different continents, in two different worlds." Mr. Tolyukov looked around the room and spread his hands apart to show two different worlds.

"Separated by a mighty ocean," said the Countess.

"Separated by the seas of God," said Tolyukov, "but brought back together again."

"But where have you been living?" Mrs. Knorr wanted to know.

"In the small town of Canaan Lake," said the Countess. "In modest circumstances."

It was Mrs. Knorr's turn to be astonished. "But that's my home!" she said. "That's where I grew up. I still have relatives there, my brother and his family."

Erikka thought suddenly: Maybe we'll visit that town someday, since Mommy has relatives there . . . back to the cabin, back to the mountain . . .

The Countess was just beginning to understand the story about the bookstore and the Pruitts. "So where do you set up shop?" she asked Tolyukov.

"I can't," he said. "I can't really afford to lose the Pruitts' business—without going to extraordinary lengths to find new customers. I'm just too old for that kind of activity. So I've closed the store down and given notice to my landlord. Without a solid bit of capital, a small business like mine would have folded anyway."

"No. I mean, money's no problem," said Olga, letting her shawl drop from her shoulders as she pulled herself to her feet. "Excuse me." She left the room.

"They just stopped where they were," Simon was saying. "They had given the check to Tolyukov and were on their way to the door when Francisco flashed in with his violin, saying, 'Mr. Tolyukov, you've just got to hear this new piece I'm learning!' And without even looking to see if Tolyukov was in the room, Francisco closed his eyes and started to play—"

"Right square in the middle of the doorway," said Tolyukov. "They would have had to run him over if they'd wanted to leave."

"But they didn't want to leave," said Simon. "At first they looked as if they would bite his head off, but then they started to listen. They closed their eyes and listened. They were spellbound."

"Mesmerized," said Tolyukov.

"Horrified, more likely," said Francisco, looking pleased. "But I'd been learning that piece for the past six months, so I really knew it. Luckily, it's written for solo violin. Otherwise they might have walked out in the orchestra parts."

"We could have done the orchestra parts," said Simon, and he began to oom-pa-pa at the top of his lungs.

"Soothing the savage beasts with music," said Tolyukov.

The Countess came back with Erikka's cloth sack. "For your family," she said to Mrs. Knorr, handing her something wrapped in paper. "From the homeland. And Modest, you must see that I am not poor. We manage. I keep some of the old things that can be sold." The Countess took off the strings of jewelry that Erikka had refused. "These will do for a time, I think."

"But why didn't you sell these things before?" Tolyukov was incredulous.

"What do I need it for? I am living a simple life in the woods," said the Countess. She smiled at Erikka. "I try to give them away once, but my friend says she has treasures already, enough for the broadness of her heart."

"We can buy that building with this," said Tolyukov. "And we can live there. And think about selling books—as we wish. Perhaps to a limited clientele."

"And Francisco next door," said the Countess. "He is our live-in med student for when we get arthritis."

"Oh, how charming," said Mrs. Knorr. She set out the present that the Countess had handed to her. It was a wooden doll, painted in bright blues and greens and reds. Annie discovered that it came apart in the middle, and that inside was another, and another, on and on, smaller and smaller, a family of ten fitting one inside the other. "Look, father, mother, and eight children." Inga lined them up.

"Here's Erikka and Inga and me and Bengt, and the new baby," said Annie, pointing. "And that leaves three left. You'll have to have three more babies, Mommy."

"A family of eight children. So many names to think of," said Mrs. Knorr, pulling Annie's thumb out of her mouth. "And now, let's have lunch. I've called Florry and told her to bring up a party platter. So we'll celebrate in style today."

"I'll pour the milk," said Annie. "Everybody else: follow me." The others followed obediently, all except Erikka and Simon and old Tolyukov.

"Erikka, your family is a treat," said Tolyukov, smiling his froggy smile. "You must count yourself blessed."

"Not usually," said Erikka.

"Well, in time you will. Time is a balm," said Tolyukov. "Think how long I had that candlestick—sixty years —before it brought me back together with the Countess. Time soothes and reveals."

"I have to give you back your candlestick," said Erikka, "now that I have the vase." She ran down the hall to her room.

On the dresser stood the old candlestick, with no candle left to burn.

Behind it was the picture, Aunt Kristina's watercolor— but the moon was no longer there. Just a clear midnight-blue sky, and a few scattered stars.

A hill. Some trees. Erikka thought as she gazed, I wonder if I will ever go there again. Time soothes and reveals, Tolyukov had said. Well, maybe time would reveal the mountain again. She picked the candlestick up and ran out, carrying it high like a torch.

After Tolyukov and the Countess had gone off, to talk and talk, and Francisco had left to study, and Simon had gone back to the school, and Inga and Annie and Bengt had gone out to play in the front, Erikka and Aunt Kristina and Mrs. Knorr did the dishes.

"She seems like a wonderful woman," said Mrs. Knorr. "Imagine being that old and all alone."

"Well, so was Tolyukov that old and all alone," said Erikka.

"I know. But now they're together, and I think it's wonderful. I didn't catch the reason she had two names, though," said Aunt Kristina.

"When she came to this country, the immigration people made the mistake. They put her middle name first and her first name middle, and they didn't even bother to try to spell 'Molokiev.' 'Maloy' was as close as they cared to come. So the Countess Olga Theresa Molokiev found on her immigration papers the name Theresa Maloy. And I guess she figured it would be easier to live with a new name than to go through the trouble of having it corrected," said Mrs. Knorr.

"I wonder what brought them together," said Aunt Kristina, drying some cups. "After all this time, I wonder what it was that reunited them?"

"Coincidence, of course. And a happy fate," said Mrs. Knorr.

Erikka wondered, too. Where was the magic in all this? Was it the candlestick, burning with the candle from a church in Old Russia? Or was it the mountainside, and the painting that Aunt Kristina had done, with the moon growing fuller and fuller?

Probably both, thought Erikka. The two good things, sitting so close together on the dresser, had acted on each other, making some magic, some strong bond, as temporary as the light of the candle and the growth of the moon to its fullness, yet still powerful. Two things kindling the magic in each other, making the union of them stronger than their individual parts, Erikka thought. Like the notes in a song. Like the colors in a painting. They're only notes and colors by themselves, but together they're songs and paintings.

But for whom had the magic been? Had it been for her? . . . or Tolyukov? . . . or the Countess? Each of the three was granted some boon: Tolyukov and the Countess were given each other; and . . . she? What was she given? She knew, but she didn't want to put it into words. Not words . . .

Mrs. Knorr (or Mommy-and-a-half, as Inga put it) turned to stack some plates. She saw the yellow roses on the table, but the peanut-butter jar was gone. In its place Erikka had put the blue vase, the cherished blue vase that had belonged to her first mother.

"Aren't you afraid that'll get broken?" said Mrs. Knorr. "You ought to be careful with it. Remember the barber's bottle!"

"I do remember. I thought we should all enjoy this one," said Erikka.

"But that belonged to Astrid, didn't it? You don't want it broken. You'll treasure it always."

"I treasure it now," said Erikka, "but I want us to enjoy it now."

"Well, it's up to you." Mrs. Knorr plunged her hands back in the dishwater. "The flowers look very nice in it."

"You've arranged them well," said Aunt Kristina, taking the dripping silver out of the bin and spreading it on the counter to pat it dry.

That evening, after Aunt Kristina had left, and Annie and Inga were moved back to their own bedroom, Erikka closed her bedroom door and sat down on the bare floor. She took out a little jar of Prussian-blue watercolor and a full brush, and leaned over a white sheet of paper. She thought hard, for a long time. Then she filled her brush with paint and held it down to the paper. Through the density of her timidity, through the thick screen of uncertainty, she leaned.

After a minute, she drew a face, a woman's face looking down on herself and on her long, full form. Inside the woman's torso she painted another face, looking up. The communication was achieved. The lines were drawn.

At the top of the page, Erikka painted a thin new moon.